GOAT IN THE GARDEN

'These two are looking for a goat,' Mr Western explained. 'You haven't seen one, have you, Dennis?'

'No, sir!' he said.

'See?' Mr Western nodded and smiled. 'Your goat isn't here. He must be halfway down to Welford by now. I should get a move on.' He closed the gates.

Mandy's head was up. Something was going on here! 'Come on!' she said to James.

They cycled until they reached the far end of the hedge.

'I don't trust them as far as I could throw them!' James said.

'Me neither. In fact, I'm really worried!' She looked anxiously at James. Houdini's footprints had come to a dead end. And she was pretty sure that Mr Western had been lying . . .

LUCY DANIELS

Goat
— *in the* —
Garden

Illustrations by Shelagh McNicholas

Hodder
Children's
Books

a division of Hodder Headline plc

Special thanks to Jenny Oldfield, and to C. J. Hall, B. Vet. Med., M.R.C.V.S. for reviewing the veterinary information contained in this book

Copyright © by Ben M. Baglio 1994
Created by Ben M. Baglio
London W6 0HE
Illustrations copyright © by Shelagh McNicholas 1994

First published in Great Britain in 1994 by Knight Books

A catalogue record for this book is available from
the British Library.

ISBN 0 340 60773 4

Typeset by Avon Dataset Ltd, Bidford-on-Avon

Printed and bound in Great Britain by
Cox & Wyman Ltd, Reading, Berkshire

Hodder Children's Books
a division of Hodder Headline plc
338 Euston Road
London NW1 3BH

To Mrs V. Morris of Town Head Farm

One

Mandy's dad was out on one of his famous jogs. He took it seriously; timed it, paced it properly, asked Mandy to ride alongside on her bicycle to give him training tips and encouragement. But still he wasn't very good.

'Lift your feet, Dad! You're running flat-footed!' Mandy sighed. At this rate he'd never be fit for the fell race.

Adam Hope lifted his feet. His breath came out in huge clouds of steam in the frosty air. With a determined look straight ahead, he tackled the long slope up out of Welford towards the Beacon.

'That's better!' Mandy encouraged, easing down

into bottom gear. The hill was a killer. Her dad's jogging action always began to look suspect at this point, and the frost underfoot was making it worse.

'Come on, Dad, you can do it!' His head was rolling from side to side. He looked desperately at his watch, but the hill was getting steeper.

'Keep going!' Mandy shouted. 'We're nearly at Beacon House. Come on!'

Mr Hope gritted his teeth.

'That's it, we're there!' The huge double gates of the Parker Smythe mansion sparkled in the clear early light. 'Take a rest, Dad.'

From here the road levelled out down a private lane to Upper Welford Hall, hidden behind tall yew hedges. Beyond that was only the Beacon itself, a Celtic cross and landmark for miles around, and one or two isolated farms. Here her dad could afford a breather.

Mr Hope collapsed forward. He bent double and gasped like a walrus. It would take about five minutes for him to recover. Meanwhile Mandy decided to potter off down the lane towards the Hall, to visit the Canada geese on the ornamental lake. 'I won't be long,' she called out.

Mr Hope raised one hand in a half-hearted wave. Mandy cycled on.

The lane was deserted. The sky was a crisp, clear

blue. Welford lay spread out like a board-game in the valley below, strange in its sparkling white coat during this late cold snap. A robin bobbed from fencepost to hedge as Mandy's bike approached. This, Mandy thought, was the perfect way to spend a Sunday morning.

'If I catch hold of that goat I'll wring its neck!' A sudden roar of rage broke the silence. It was nearby. It was loud. It was frightening. 'Grab it, Dennis! Good Lord, man, grab the darned thing!'

It was on the far side of the hedge. There were noises, tramplings, shovings and more outraged roars. 'Now look! Look what you've done! You've let it get near the house!'

Curiosity overcame fear, and Mandy pedalled for the gap in the hedge. What was going on? Who was shouting? What goat was this?

She peered over a low wooden gate marked 'Private' on to the perfect landscaped gardens of Upper Welford Hall. Every bush, every shrub was clipped and knew its place. Every pear tree was neatly pinned to a wall, every weeping willow knew to weep over its special bit of water.

There were ponds and stone statues; there were paths to sundials; there were low walls and hedges, grassy slopes and empty but perfectly dug flower-beds still caught in the grip of this late snowfall.

And there by the main entrance to the lovely old Hall was the goat!

'Stop it!' the same man was roaring. 'Dennis, it's eating the ivy!' He stood on the vast front lawn, waving his arms. 'I tell you I'll wring its neck!'

Dennis was creeping up on the goat from behind. The goat was black as tar. The drive and front steps were frosty white. The goat reached up for a choice nibble of tender ivy shoot. It pretended not to notice Dennis.

Dennis, in overalls and a blue anorak, seemed to think all fours was best for catching goats. He put up a warning hand to tell the roaring man to be quiet. The goat munched on.

There was not much green about for a goat to munch at this time of year, and the ivy was a special treat. Mandy watched him, admiring his graceful head, his long legs.

Dennis crept forward. He lunged. Nimbly the goat sidestepped and Dennis fell flat on the gravel drive. Mandy put a hand to her mouth. Now was not the time to laugh out loud.

'Good Lord!' the angry man cried. He was red in the face. The wind caught and ruffled his carefully combed quiff of grey-blond hair. He watched in dismay as the black goat skittered sideways and headed for the fresh ivy on the far side of the imposing stone doorway.

But now the two men abandoned caution and went for the more direct approach. No more stalking their quarry. No, this time they charged, one from each side, running full-tilt towards the quietly grazing animal.

Mandy glanced sideways. Her dad had come up the lane to find her. 'Shh!' she said, pointing.

They watched a kind of cartoon ballet in the white garden. Men lunged, goat danced sideways. Men ran and waved their arms, goat shook his head and skipped out of reach. Men pursued goat. Goat kicked his heels, crashed through a tiny hedge across a bed of rhododendrons. Deep footmarks everywhere. Men fell down on frosty slope. Goat swooped downhill toward willows by pond; willow, like ivy, was clearly a favourite treat.

'Uh-oh!' Mr Hope said, seeing ahead to the next move.

'Shh!' Mandy warned. Somehow she wanted the goat to win. Not that she had anything against the men. She just naturally sided with animals every time. 'Look, he's going to get away!'

The men charged down the icy slope. The goat munched its willow twig. It glanced sideways, shook its head and deftly sidestepped once more.

The men roared out of control. They skidded, slipped and slid down the final few metres. They grabbed whatever they could to stop themselves, but it was only each other. And together they crashed into the icy pond, shrieking and yelling.

'Ha!' Mandy couldn't help it. She laughed into her tartan woollen scarf. Canada geese flapped noisily across the pond, while the goat capered off up the slope, leaving the men wet and stranded.

'Come on!' Mr Hope ordered. 'Let's head it off!'

They could tell that the goat's direction was down the main drive. With luck they would get to it as it reached the gate, and its fun would be over.

'Who does he belong to?' Mandy whispered as they ran. 'Do you know?'

Her dad shook his head. 'No, I've never seen him before. But we'd better get hold of him before those two do, and see if we can get him back to his proper owner. I wouldn't fancy being in this goat's shoes if Dennis and his boss get there first!'

They reached the gate and stood there legs apart, arms stretched wide in a human barrier. The goat saw them, pulled up short and set up a loud, mad bleating. He shot a glance behind at the enraged, dripping men still clambering out of the pond. Then common sense overcame him. He stopped bleating, lowered his head, and gentle as a lamb he walked straight into Mandy's open arms.

'Here, boy. Here, then!' she breathed. She had fallen straight away for the goat's beautiful green eyes. His face was clever. He was magnificent. 'Here!' she coaxed. He would let her stroke him and take him by the collar. He would allow her to lead him off to safety! She beamed at her father.

'You go on; you seem to have a way with him,' Mr Hope said. 'I'll stay here and have a word.' And he stepped in between the beautiful black goat and its pursuers. 'Hello, I'm Adam Hope from Animal Ark,' he said pleasantly. 'I see you've been having a spot of trouble.'

Mandy didn't wait to hear the rest of the conversation. Proudly she led the goat on down the lane.

At the spot where she'd left her bike, Mandy waited. She let the goat nuzzle at her pockets, enjoying the feel of its soft nose and its giant set of bottom teeth. She scratched its bony forehead and looked into its big green eyes. The long black coat was shiny and soft, the back was strong and straight. Obviously this goat was well looked after.

'Now who do you belong to?' she said, settling down beside the goat on the frosty roadside. She reached for the metal tag on its rough leather collar. There was writing on it, but it was difficult to read;

not engraved but scratched on to the metal in awkward handwriting. Mandy screwed up her eyes and concentrated. 'Houdini', she read. And underneath, 'High Cross Farm'. Mandy pulled a face. 'Never heard of it', she said to herself.

Then her dad came jogging down the lane, a sprightly spring back in his step.

'What happened?' Mandy asked. She settled a nervous Houdini with 'Shh, there's a good boy. It's only my dad!'

'What do you mean, "only"?' Mr Hope asked, but he was wearing his lopsided grin.

'Nice goat,' he said appreciatively. 'Slim shoulders, wide hips, strong legs, good feet. British Alpine breed. Hmm!' He ran his eye over Houdini. 'Good pedigree!'

Mandy was impressed. 'I never knew you knew so much about goats.'

'I did a special study at college, way back,' Mr Hope said. 'Not a lot of call for it at Animal Ark of course. But it comes in handy now and again.'

'Like now?'

He nodded. Houdini lifted his head and gave a horsey snicker. Then he nosed in Mr Hope's tracksuit where he found a half-eaten Mars bar. It was gone almost before Mandy had time to recognise what it was.

'Dad!' she protested. 'How could you? That's hundreds of calories!'

'Energy,' Mr Hope explained. 'I need energy!'

Houdini gulped and swallowed, then tried the other pocket.

'Anyway,' Mandy said, 'what did happen with those two men?'

'Ah!' Mr Hope shook his head. 'Those two men, as you call them, didn't appreciate this goat's fine pedigree, beauty and intelligence.' He was grinning again. 'In fact I recognised Sam Western by his voice, and Dennis Saville is his estate manager. I know him from the Fox and Goose.'

'And what did they say to you?'

Mr Hope raised one eyebrow. ' "If that goat comes near my garden just one more time I won't answer for the consequences!" Or words to that effect.'

Mandy felt a little surge of anger in her throat. She hated it when anyone threatened a defenceless animal. 'Huh!' She looked Houdini in the face. 'They'd better not try anything with you,' she said stubbornly. Then she turned to her dad. 'What do you think they would do to him?'

He shrugged. 'Shoot him. Poison him. Who knows? They're not animal lovers, that's for sure.'

Mandy gasped. 'But they live in the country. They must like animals!' She couldn't believe that people who lived with beautiful creatures day in day out could harbour a single cruel thought towards them.

Mr Hope tried to explain, though Houdini was getting restless. He skittered sideways with his back legs and blew noisily into the frosty air. Soon they would have to decide a plan of action. 'Sam Western's a dairy farmer as a matter of fact. Upper Welford Hall may look ancient, but behind this old house lie the farm buildings and they run like clockwork, I can tell you. Modern machinery. Minimum labour, maximum yield. He's the type who probably wishes his cows could be mechanical too!'

Houdini lifted his head and showed his teeth. 'Quite right,' Mr Hope said. 'As Houdini says, "Bah!" '

They laughed. 'Anyway, love, you'd better hang on here with this chap while I borrow your bike and dash back down to the Ark.' Mr Hope took a quick look at Houdini's tag. 'I'll try to find this High Cross Farm on a map and drive back up with the Land-rover to take old Houdini safely back home. OK? Think you can manage that?'

Mandy nodded. 'I think we can, don't you, Houdini?'

She could have sworn that the animal nodded its head. So she and Houdini watched Mr Hope career down the road, skidding at icy corners and snaking round hairpin bends towards Animal Ark.

Then silence. Nothing but miles of blue sky and white fields. Mandy felt tiny, perched up here on the hillside. Houdini looked again at Mandy. Did he grin?

Anyway, he decided that waiting on a cold hillside with nothing better to chew on than the fringe on Mandy's woollen scarf was not his idea of fun. Mandy still held his collar, but he wrenched his neck sideways. She clung on, but Houdini was on the move and there was nothing she could do about it.

'Steady boy!' she said. He might as well have been deaf. He set off at a brisk trot up the lane again, dragging Mandy along with him. She was surprised by his strength.

'Oh, no!' Mandy saw the Hall gates loom. She remembered Mr Western's angry threat. She had visions of shotguns at the ready, but she breathed a sigh of relief when Houdini managed to ignore the temptations of willow and ivy. He trotted purposefully on.

'Thank heavens!' she said. They'd been in enough trouble with Mr Western for one day already.

Up the hill they trotted, with the Beacon perched on top. Up an unmade road with an old wooden fingerpost to point the way. 'High Cross Farm' it said in faded letters. 'Good boy!' Mandy said. He was finding his own way home!

Soon she could see a building at the end of the track,

still higher, still more remote. It seemed safe to let the goat run free now, so Mandy released her hold on his collar. He hesitated, gave a little kick of his back legs, then trotted on. Mandy followed. She wanted to be sure he didn't take another detour. She wanted him safely home.

And in a strange way Houdini seemed to be wanting her to accompany him right up to the farm. He kept an eye on her, waited a second or two, nodded and trotted on, so they arrived at High Cross together.

'Good boy!' Mandy said one last time. No need for the map or the Land-rover after all. 'Well done!'

She opened the old five-barred gate by lifting a loop of frayed rope attached to the gatepost, then she helped the gate creak on its hinges. There was an overgrown path up the final fifty metres to the old farmhouse.

It was a tiny place perched on the hill, sheltered by stunted hawthorns all leaning at an impossible angle after years in the fierce north wind. Moss covered the stone walls of the house and crept on to the roof. The windows looked blind and empty. The front door, once red, hadn't been painted for years. To one side of the house stood a long, low barn, windowless and gloomy. To the other was a set of ramshackle outbuildings. Nothing moved. There was no sound. For a moment Mandy thought the place was deserted.

But Houdini trotted confidently on. Mandy followed him up the path.

Eagerly now the goat put on a little burst of speed, cutting across the small courtyard and down by the side of the barn. Behind the house the farmland fell away into the next valley; mile upon mile of new white fields, black outcrops of rock, a silver river winding in the valley bottom.

Nearer at hand Mandy could hear the sound of running water. She saw Houdini head for the stream, frisky as ever. Soon she caught sight of it and could see that it was partly frozen over. She heard ice being broken and then at last she saw a figure astride the stream. It was crouched over, using the base of a metal bucket to hammer away at the splintering ice.

The person was completely absorbed in breaking the ice and gathering fresh water. At first glance Mandy took it for a boy, sturdy and short haired, muffled in an old brown jacket. But no, something in the movements told her it was a woman who broke the ice and dipped the bucket in the clear water.

The woman must have heard Houdini's firm, crisp tread. Mandy saw her raise her head. The face broke into a broad, clear smile. She stood up, hands on hips astride the stream. 'So!' she said with great delight. 'If it isn't old Houdini! You did it again, found your own way home!' She shook her head and laughed.

Then she saw Mandy and the smile vanished from her face.

Two

All Mandy's bright confidence slipped away. She'd expected a thank you and a wave, but the look on the woman's face was pure dismay. She clutched the top of her scruffy jacket, pulling the collar close to her face. On her hands she wore black fingerless gloves. The elbows on her jacket were worn clean through and her corduroy trousers were bald at the knees. Bits of string held things together round her waist. She was a mess, Mandy decided. What's more, she didn't welcome visitors to High Cross.

'Sorry!' Mandy half smiled and backed away. 'I didn't mean to make you jump.' She was wondering how a goat as bright and comical as Houdini could possibly have such a strange owner.

The woman just stared, bucket at her feet, with the icy water of the stream splashing against her wellingtons. The goat nudged her, half overbalancing her.

'I — we found Houdini in the garden of the Hall,' Mandy stumbled on. 'I brought him home for you.'

The woman stared and nodded. It was as close as she would get to saying thank you, so Mandy shuffled backwards, ready to depart. But Houdini caught her eye. As always, her love of anything to do with animals rose to the surface. 'Why is he called Houdini?' she blurted out.

And it was as if a dam had burst. The smile came back on the woman's face and the words poured out. 'Ah, it's because he's always escaping from impossible situations. Like the great Houdini, the escapologist, in the old days. He was always escaping from chains. I tether that goat, I chain him, I lock him up in his pen. I mend all the holes in the wall. But nothing stops Houdini! I tempt him with the best meadow hay from the top meadow, I feed him the best greens, but nothing contents this fellow, does it, boy?'

The goat put up his head haughtily and laughed.

The woman laughed back. 'Yes, he's a devil for escaping, is Houdini!'

Mandy's own awkwardness melted in this shared

admiration for the goat. 'He's beautiful,' she said. 'Even if he is a bit frisky!'

The woman laughed richly. 'Frisky! He's a stubborn, mad old thing. He jumps everything I put up to keep him in, chews everything I use to tie him up.' She scratched her head and sighed. 'Of course, it's a problem,' she admitted.

Mandy felt brave enough to come forward and pat Houdini. Really, the woman was quite friendly after all, if you managed to get on the right side of her. She might look odd, with her boyish haircut and her jumble-sale clothes, but she knew how to treat her goat. 'What's a problem?' Mandy asked.

'The fencing.' She cast an arm towards the broken-down stone walls and the makeshift wire netting fences. 'I try my best. But bad fences make bad neighbours pretty quickly, as they say!'

Mandy remembered Mr Western and nodded. 'Do you live here all by yourself?' she asked. 'Isn't there anyone to rebuild the walls?' They were crumbling back into jumbled piles of stones, easy for a goat to jump.

'Just me,' the woman said.

Mandy looked again. Why did she live alone? Was she a widow? She must be about fifty, though the clothes and the roughly cut grey hair made it difficult to tell.

'Just me. And the goats, of course,' she added.

Mandy's eyes lit up. 'You've got other goats?' she asked. Then she remembered her manners. 'Oh, by the way, I'm Mandy Hope. I'm the vets' daughter from Welford. From Animal Ark!'

'Well!' the woman said slowly, as if she was making a decision. She had a smile hovering about her mouth. 'In that case you'd better come and see the herd.'

And she climbed up the bank from the stream with her full bucket, leading the way back to the farm. 'It's only a small herd, mind you, though the goats will be ready to kid this spring, and I have three kids just now. I don't let them breed, of course. I stick to British Alpines. I like the breed because they have personality — a bit of something about them if you see what I mean.'

Mandy glanced at wicked Houdini and nodded in agreement.

They trudged through ankle-deep hoar frost, making a trail over the field. Again the words poured out, unstoppable. If it was to do with goats, the woman seemed to forget everything else. Then suddenly she stopped, gave Houdini a little thwack on his rump to send him on his way into the yard, turned back to Mandy and gave a formal little bow.

'You must think me very rude,' she said. 'Only I don't get many visitors, being so cut off.' She cleared her throat. 'I'm Lydia Fawcett. I'm pleased to meet you.' And she put out a hand.

Mandy shook her hand warmly. 'And do the goats stay indoors for the winter?' she asked as they tramped on, glad that the frosty reception had melted away.

'Oh, yes. Goats hate the damp. They panic in the rain. And they absolutely detest the cold. Here!' Lydia strode ahead and lifted the latch on a small door set into the huge dilapidated double door of the barn. Mandy followed her, stooped and stepped inside.

The barn was arranged in two rows of pens with a walkway down the middle. It was dusty and dark, but the feel and sound of contented animals was strong. The place was airy and warm, despite the cold outside, for the stone walls were sturdy and the floor was deep in clean straw.

Mandy watched as Lydia poured fresh water into the drinking pails outside each pen. She saw with delight that at each splash a goat popped its head quickly through a keyhole-shaped opening in the front of the pen. They drank noisily and thirstily.

'How many are there?' she asked, making a fuss of Houdini. He'd come up to investigate her pockets once more.

'Twelve. A nice size for a herd.' Lydia had taken a pitchfork from a corner and thrust it into a stack of sweet-smelling hay. 'Though I confess that twelve take some feeding through the winter!'

She dropped hay alongside each water pail, and again the goats' heads appeared to set up a loud munching. Lydia sighed and replaced the pitchfork. 'Goats eat so much bulk. It's the fresh greens,' she explained. 'So expensive.' She looked sad and worried.

Mandy looked at the well-kept barn, its neat rows of pens, the old-fashioned farm tools stacked in one corner and hung in rows along the far wall. 'I suppose that's why Houdini keeps escaping?' she asked, recalling the fresh ivy shoots growing up the front walls of Upper Welford Hall.

Lydia dipped a big metal scoop into a wooden bin and began sharing out a mixture of oats and barley. The goats snickered with pleasure and tucked in again. 'Was Mr Western very angry?' she asked quietly.

Mandy nodded. 'Oh, yes, purple. Fuming. He fell into the pond.' She tried to keep a straight face.

'Oh, my!' Lydia said, with a look of alarm. Then she burst into a peal of laughter. 'Oh, Houdini! The billy-goats are the worst for wandering off. It's a good job I've only got two to worry about!'

She led him into his pen, fed and watered him, gave him a final look over in case of damage, and led

Mandy out of the barn. She bolted the door with care. 'You see,' she said, 'I do take great care to stop his jaunts!'

But Mandy was too full of her own questions to agree. 'When do you milk the goats? How often? Is it difficult?' she said in a rush.

'Whoa!' Lydia said, halfway across the yard towards the house. 'Too many questions. You'd better come inside and let me make us a cup of tea!'

They opened the faded red door and stepped inside the house.

It was like going through a time warp, stepping back into the past. There was no fridge, no cooker, no washing-machine. The cupboards were old and battered. Great beams supported the ceiling. And books crowded all the surfaces — shelves, tables, windowsills. Some had even toppled on to the floor.

Mandy sat down at a huge scrubbed table and watched Lydia poke at the embers of a fire in the old iron kitchen range. She shook coal on to it out of a battered black bucket, tended the fire, then went to fill a kettle at the shallow sink by the window. She set it on a hob and swung the whole thing over the fire. Then she bustled about in cupboards for cups and saucers. 'No cake, I'm afraid,' she apologised as finally the tea arrived in chipped cups that didn't quite match the saucers.

Mandy moved closer to the fire with her cup of tea while Lydia explained the milking routine. 'Twice daily summer and winter, seven days a week in all weathers. And of course,' Lydia said, 'the milk is delicious.'

She went to a high cupboard and fetched a clean jamjar. She dipped a ladle into a metal churn set on the windowsill over the sink and scooped out the creamy liquid. Carefully she poured and then turned the screw cap on the jar. 'Here,' she said to Mandy with a shy smile. 'Take some home and try it.'

Mandy remembered 'home' with a start. She'd been so caught up in the herd of goats that she'd forgotten her dad. He must be just about to set out looking for her and the goat. She jumped up. 'Can I phone my dad, please?'

'I'm sorry, I don't have a phone,' Lydia said. 'No television, no radio. I do have running water and electricity,' she said proudly.

Mandy stared. She'd never heard of anyone being able to manage without a radio at least.

'My father was maybe a bit old-fashioned about such things, right up until he died,' Lydia explained. 'He didn't believe in modern gadgets. The old way was good enough. He lived in this house all his life and he saw no reason to alter things. But he did like to have the water laid on, and the light at the flick of a switch. So he put in the pipes and so on. And very glad I am too!' She sat by the fire, cosy and content.

'But how do you make arrangements without a telephone? I mean, what if there's an emergency?'

Lydia shook her head. 'I don't have the need, touch wood. I live simply, as you see. And it suits me.'

She sat there in the middle of her stone-flagged kitchen floor in her wellington boots and old clothes. Mandy guessed that Lydia hadn't bought a single scrap of clothing for herself or a single teaspoon for the house for at least ten years.

'Well,' Mandy said, caught up in the wonder of it all, 'I'd best be off.' She got up to go, but she could hear that a car was on its way up to High Cross. She recognised the sound of the Land-rover, its engine whining up the hill. 'That must be my dad now,' she said.

At once the smile vanished from Lydia's face. It closed down and a look of suspicion replaced it.

'He must have found High Cross on the map and guessed I'd be up here with Houdini,' she explained. 'Come on, come and meet him!'

'He's a veterinary, you say?' Lydia stacked the cups slowly in the stone sink.

'Yes. At Animal Ark in Welford. He runs the practice, along with my mother.'

She shook her head. 'I don't generally hold with veterinaries.'

Mandy read between the lines: Lydia had no money to pay vets' fees. She was quickly learning to pick up real meanings beneath Lydia's old-fashioned phrases. 'Oh, come on, he'd love to see the goats. He's a goat expert!' she said proudly.

And that was just enough to break the shell of Lydia's shyness. They went out together to greet Mr Hope and Mandy's friend, James Hunter, at the ancient wooden gate.

'Dad, James! Houdini got impatient waiting. He found his own way home! And this is Lydia. Lydia Fawcett, and she runs a goat farm all by herself, way up here, and she'd like to show you her goats, wouldn't you, Lydia? And they're absolutely brilliant. And, Lydia, this is my dad and my friend, James Hunter. James, what are you doing here?' Mandy said, almost without pausing.

'Not so fast,' Mr Hope said. He politely shook hands with Lydia. James couldn't help staring at the odd figure and he raised his eyebrows at Mandy. 'I'm sure Miss Fawcett doesn't want to be bothered,' her dad said.

'Oh, no, not at all. You're welcome to see the goats,' Lydia said.

While the grown-ups went through the usual politenesses, Mandy told James a bit about High Cross. 'There's no telephone . . . no TV,' she whispered as they crossed the yard towards the barn. 'Isn't it great?'

James fixed his glasses more firmly on his nose. She could see he was about to disagree. 'What's great about no TV?'

'There are books!' Mandy said. Lydia had stacks of them, even in her kitchen, on the mantelpiece over the cooking range, in alcoves, everywhere.

James just shook his head.

They'd reached the barn now. Lydia went in and unlatched the door of the nearest pen. She led out a lovely black and white goat for Mr Hope to see. She was medium size, sleek, with two white stripes down her face. Her beard was pure white.

Mr Hope ran an eye over her. He felt her silky coat and made murmuring sounds of approval. 'Lovely,' he said. 'Lovely pedigree, lovely condition. You should show her this spring in the village show.'

'Oh, no,' Lydia said, overcome with modesty. 'I shouldn't think of doing that.'

Mr Hope nodded quietly, peering into each pen. 'Nice,' he said each time. Or, 'Very nice!'

Mandy felt pleased as punch. She already felt proud of Lydia's goats!

'And you manage to kid them yourself?' he asked, as he looked into the last pen.

Lydia nodded. 'It's generally pretty straight-forward.'

'Well, if you ever need a hand just give me a shout,' he offered.

Lydia withdrew half a step and put on a slightly more formal tone. 'That's very kind of you,' she said, 'but I think I shall manage.'

'Well,' Mr Hope insisted, 'if you ever need anything, we're just down in the village.'

'Dad!' Mandy cut in. Things were getting awkward. Mr Hope didn't understand that Lydia had no money and was too proud to mention it.

Lydia was looking more withdrawn. She drew herself together with great dignity inside her shabby brown jacket. 'I thank you,' she said, very stiff, very distant. 'But I don't need anything. As I was saying, I've lived here all my life, Mr Hope, and I've never had to rely on help or advice. I run my little herd very happily by myself, thank you.'

Mandy put a hand on her dad's shoulder, ready to make a quiet, quick exit. But Lydia hadn't finished.

She raised her chin, squared her shoulders. 'I ask very little,' she said in a clear, firm tone, ignoring Mandy now. 'But I do ask one thing, and that is to be left alone!'

And with that she showed them out of the barn, down the cobbled path. She stood at the gate and watched them climb into the Land-rover.

Mandy cringed as her dad went back for a final word. She wound down the window to listen. 'I say,' he said, his usual, straightforward self. 'I did mean to mention one thing; it's about Houdini.'

'Well?' Lydia said, still suspicious.

'Well, Sam Western's in a rage about the state of his garden, and you know what he's like.' He paused. 'It's not the first time old Houdini's made a mess of his flower-beds, apparently.'

Lydia met his gaze with a steely stare.

'Anyway, he's pushing his weight around, saying he'll take definite action next time.'

Silence. Lydia made no move. She didn't even blink.

'I'm just mentioning it. If I were you, I'd keep the old boy a bit more secure just in case!'

'You're not me, Mr Hope,' Lydia said at last. She rammed the loop of rope firmly over the gatepost.

Mandy waved, but Lydia ignored her again, as Mr Hope climbed in and the Land-rover slid downhill towards the road.

'What did I say?' Mandy's dad asked, scratching his beard. 'What made her go off like that?'

Mandy sensed but she couldn't tell him. It had hurt Lydia's pride, that offer of help. Vets cost money. The drugs and the X-rays are expensive. There was no way that Lydia could afford to take Mr Hope up on his offer. 'Oh, nothing, Dad,' she said.

Mr Hope frowned. 'One very peculiar lady,' he said.

'No, she's not!' Mandy snapped. She felt sad. And she felt confused. Why was she angry with her own father?

The three of them sat in silence all the way home.

Three

Back at Animal Ark Mandy offered James a drink of goats' milk from the jar. 'Well?' she asked, keen to share her new love for goats with him.

He wrinkled his nose. His face went red to the roots of his short brown hair. When he spoke his voice sounded strange. 'I know I ought to like it . . .'

'But?' Mandy grabbed it from him, determined to say it was the most delicious thing she'd ever tasted. She drank down a gulp of the creamy white milk. 'Wonderful!' she said. But even she had to admit to herself that the taste was rich and strange.

'I suppose I could get used to it,' was all James could manage to say.

Mandy shot him a challenging glance. 'Say what you really think, James Hunter. Go on!'

James screwed up his face. 'OK then: yuk!'

Mandy laughed. 'Well, it says here in my dad's old college book on goats that goats' milk is good for you. It can help with asthma, eczema and stomach disorders. And that's not just old wives' tales.' She passed over the book, still eager for James to share her excitement. 'In Asia Minor,' she said, pointing at the page over his shoulder, 'they found a man who was one hundred and eighty years old and he only ever drank goats' milk. See!'

James wasn't impressed. 'Where's Asia Minor?' he asked.

'I don't know.' Mandy took back the book and slammed it shut. She put the jamjar of milk in the fridge. 'But I know that from now on I'm never going to drink anything else!'

James leaned on the kitchen table and did a quick sum in his head. 'In that case you should still be alive in one hundred and sixty-eight years' time!' he said.

Mandy flung a round cracker towards him. 'Here, catch!' she said. James didn't. 'A pity my dad and Lydia didn't hit it off.' She munched slowly. 'Still, never mind. I think I'll cycle up there tomorrow straight after school, to take her jamjar back. Do you want to come?' Secretly, Mandy couldn't wait to get back up to High Cross to visit Lydia and her goats again.

'To take her jamjar back?' James echoed in disbelief. 'I know we recycle everything and all that, but isn't that a bit much? Why not just take it to the bottle bank?'

Mandy sighed. Sometimes she had to spell things out. 'It's an excuse, see! To go back to High Cross! To see Houdini!'

James grinned. 'I knew that, stupid! I just wanted to make you say it!'

And she chased him round the table, laughing.

Mandy and James went up to Lydia's next day to return the jar. Mandy was nervous as she lifted the loop of rope on the old gate at High Cross. Would Lydia still be angry? Would she still say that she just wanted to be left alone?

They found her in the barn, hard at work cleaning out the goat pens. 'Come on, Jemima, come on, girl!' She coaxed the goat out of the pen, glanced up and saw James and Mandy. 'Hello there,' she said briskly.

'We've brought this back,' Mandy said, timidly holding up the clean jar.

'Well, thank you very much!' Lydia stood up straight. She smiled at them, and all their shy feelings vanished. 'Now that you're here, why not make yourselves useful?' she asked.

Mandy grinned at James.

'Take Jemima for me, please. Hold on to her and let me introduce you to some of the others. That one next door is Lady Jayne, and this one's Olivia.' Lydia began to count off the goats in their pens. 'That little one opposite is Monty, the other billy-goat. He's one of my favourites!'

Mandy and James listened and nodded. Once Lydia had finished the list of names, they willingly agreed to help fill the food buckets with oats and barley.

Each goat bobbed its head through the keyhole gap and gobbled eagerly.

'That's right! The best way to a goat's heart is through his stomach!' Lydia said with a laugh.

In the next week or two, while the late cold snap still held the countryside in its grip, Mandy and James got to know everything about goats. They went up regularly to High Cross and learned to muck out the pens and lay down clean straw. Then they watched Lydia to learn how to milk.

Lydia welcomed them each time with her special smile. 'Stand clear,' she said, leading one of the goats back into a clean pen. 'Steady, Jemima, steady, girl!'

Mandy found she could recognise Jemima by the

long thin stripe of white down her back. She watched as Lydia hedged the goat in against a side wall, her head in the far corner. Then Lydia placed a metal pail under the udder and squeezed with each hand in a rhythmical, strong downwards movement. Jemima never stirred. 'Good girl,' Lydia said as the white liquid foamed into the bucket.

'Is it easy?' Mandy asked. She'd seen cows being milked in huge milking parlours, attached to machines with long tubes from udder to plastic container. But this hand milking looked a much bigger challenge.

'Here,' Lydia offered unexpectedly, moving off the stool. By now she readily gave them jobs, trusted them near her precious animals. 'Give over, Jemima,' she said as the goat lifted a back leg. And she sat Mandy down on the stool. 'Go on; you have to squeeze one finger at a time in quick succession, not all at once, from the top finger down. That's it, give it a go!'

Mandy took a deep breath and rested one shoulder against Jemima's flank. She followed instructions, clumsily at first. To her surprise, the milk began to flow into the bucket.

'That's it,' Lydia said, nodding. 'It's a bit slow until you're used to it, and you're lucky she's a good milker. Not bad for a first effort!'

Mandy frowned with concentration. But as the milk flowed she felt pleased with her success. 'Good girl,

Jemima,' she said softly. Then she stood up, took the bucket over to a metal churn and tipped the contents in, as Lydia had done. She filtered the milk in through a strainer, then closed the lid of the churn.

'It'll cool fast enough in this weather without running it under cold water.' Lydia busied herself at the next pen. 'Steady, Alexandra,' she said as she opened the next door. Then she turned to James. 'Your turn now!'

James shot Mandy a panicky look, but there was no room to argue with Lydia. Bravely he entered Alexandra's pen.

Lydia was firm and patient. 'That's right,' she said. 'Now remember what I've told you!'

Alexandra behaved sweetly as James sat down and began to milk. She never shifted until he'd finished. At last he emerged with the bucket, grinning at Mandy, and tipped the milk into the churn.

Together they went out to the stream for fresh water for the goats.

'Great, isn't it?' Mandy asked, looking down the rolling dale to the distant river. 'I mean, how can people possibly not like goats?'

James nodded. By now he was a goat fan too!

The thaw was late coming to Welford and even later up at High Cross, where the frost hung on and snow drifts lingered in the shaded side of the blackened drystone walls.

And Mandy noticed every time she visited Lydia that her stock of hay was less, the levels in her great bins of cereals and concentrates even lower. Still there was no fresh pasture to turn the goats on to, and the wind whistled round the Beacon as if it was the North Pole. Day by day, Mandy grew more anxious for Lydia and her goats.

Lydia would shake her head, her own face pinched with cold and worry. The goats were perfectly kept, but Mandy couldn't help looking at her and feeling worried.

'I don't know,' Lydia said. It was early one Saturday. 'Sometimes I wonder how many more winters I can last. Especially long hard ones like this one.' She was standing at the barn door, staring out at the empty, grey, cobbled yard. 'It's the winters that will beat me in the end.'

'Oh, no!' Mandy said. A terrible panic shot through her. Lydia mustn't give up. What would happen to her goats? And what would happen to Lydia? 'Don't say that! I'm sure things will work out OK!'

But for the moment Lydia refused to cheer up. 'I'm clean out of kale and greens of all kinds. I'm nearly out of hay, as you see. Poor beasts, they'll starve one of these days!' Then briskly she turned, went back inside and checked Houdini's door. 'Steady boy!' Houdini popped his head over the stable door and gave Mandy a knowing look.

'But you can get more food to see you through the last bit of winter,' Mandy said, trying to be bright and practical. 'Couldn't you buy some bulk turnips or potatoes?'

Lydia gave her a glance that spoke volumes. 'When the goats finally come to kid next month, then I shall have some stock to sell on. I shan't like to part with a single one of them of course, but I shall find good homes, and some folk are willing to pay a fair price for a good kid these days.'

Mandy realised how stupid she'd been to think Lydia could afford extra food for the goats. They'd simply have to hang on until the cold snap ended.

'Where does the milk go to?' James asked, quick to change the subject. He helped fasten the latch on the top part of Houdini's stable door, then Lydia herself locked the outer barn door. They tramped together across the yard, stamping their feet in the cold.

'The milk's collected every third day.' Lydia took them over to an outhouse beyond the farmhouse itself. She opened the door and pointed inside to a dozen or more metal churns. 'This is the cool house. Mr Wintersgill from down the dale calls up here to collect sixteen gallons at a time.' She closed the door. 'He has a cheese factory over in Thirsk. He pays me one pound fifty a gallon,' she announced.

James and Mandy did their sums. This meant that Lydia's income was over fifty pounds a week.

'My father would never have believed it!' Lydia said. 'Milk fetched one shilling and sixpence when he was alive, and he never thought much of goatkeeping to earn a living. Of course feeding a goat is expensive. People think they'll eat any old thing, but they're very particular. A goat won't eat anything soiled or second-rate.'

Lydia chatted as she showed them down to the gate.

James and Mandy turned to say goodbye, but instead an extraordinary sight caught their eye.

'Look!' Mandy pointed to the barn. 'Up on the roof!'

They looked again. There was no mistake. Caught in perfect silhouette against the grey sky, staring grandly down from the roof, was a goat!

'Houdini!' Lydia shouted, recognising him at once. 'Come straight down here!'

'How did he get up there?' Mandy gasped. He was seven metres up, standing like the king of the world on the sharp ridge of the roof.

'You monkey!' Lydia called, really cross. She strode back up the path, her brown jacket flapping open. 'He probably climbed out of his pen!'

James went red and hot. It had been his job to leave Houdini safely locked in there.

'No, no, it's not your fault,' Lydia said. 'Don't you worry, he's very clever at getting out, just like his namesake. Once he's headbutted and nibbled his way out of his pen, he uses the meal bins as a step up into the hayloft. Then he squeezes out of the narrow window and mountaineers up the outside wall of the barn and on to the roof! And there you are!' She stood staring up at Houdini, but he only returned the stare defiantly. 'Come down!' she called again, shaking her fist.

But Houdini had tasted freedom.

'Why does he climb up there?' Mandy said, amazed.

'He's looking for food, I'm afraid,' Lydia said. Houdini tapped a hoof impatiently on the ridge tile, planning his best escape route.

'There he goes!' Mandy yelled, watching the black silhouette vanish nimbly down the far side of the long roof. They heard only the clatter of hooves, then silence.

They ran and scrambled round the side of the barn, only to see Houdini already making off into the distance, over one low wall, across a meadow, up to a section of wire fence. A stubborn look came over him.

His head went down and he charged the fencepost. He withdrew, charged again. At the third charge, just as they had him almost within their grasp, the fencepost toppled and Houdini nipped through. Between him and the wide world nothing now stood in his way!

'Houdini!' Lydia muttered. 'Drat!'

'Don't worry, we'll catch him for you,' Mandy said. Like James, she felt that it was partly their fault that Houdini had escaped this time.

Lydia gave her a weary look. 'You can try,' she said, 'but I've more milking to do, if you'll excuse me.' And she turned to go.

'Lydia!' Mandy protested. 'You can't just leave him to wander!' Again the picture of Sam Western and Dennis Saville, shotguns at the ready, flashed before her eyes.

'And I can't just leave goats in the barn that need milking,' Lydia explained. 'That's what's so hard about running a farm by yourself. The goats get uncomfortable and unhappy if they're not milked on time.' She sighed, looking up and down the track for any sign of Houdini. 'No, I'm afraid we'll just have to wait until he makes his own way back, or until I've finished the milking!' She shook her head.

'But what about Mr Western?' Mandy asked. How could Lydia take this so calmly?

Lydia paused and considered. 'I just hope he'll have more sense.'

'Who, Mr Western?'

'No, Houdini,' Lydia said finally as she went back to her work.

'What shall we do?' Mandy watched the retreating figure. They'd lost sight of the goat long since.

'Follow him!' James said promptly.

And they were on their bikes, riding the rough lane before they had any more time to think.

'What now?' James asked as the gates of Upper Welford Hall loomed. Great swirls of grey cloud were settling on the hills all around, threatening rain or maybe even snow.

Mandy dismounted from her bike and concentrated on the grass verge alongside the tall hedge surrounding Mr Western's property. And sure enough, there were the telltale cloven hoofmarks. 'He's been through this way!' she said, excitement strangling her voice. 'But the hoofmarks finish right here, see!'

Mandy felt like Sherlock Holmes as she and James crouched to examine the ground.

'Well, well,' said a voice. 'And what can I do for you two?'

They looked up. The voice belonged to Mr

Western. Mandy didn't feel like Sherlock Holmes any more — more like a little girl caught with her fingers in the sweet jar. 'Er . . .' she said, standing up straight. She felt very red and hot.

'Um . . .' James stood too and fiddled with the bridge of his glasses.

But to their surprise Mr Western was looking pleasant and relaxed. He pressed a button and the iron gates swung open. He stepped outside, hands behind his back, immaculate in his green waxed jacket and stylish haircut. 'Let me guess,' he said. 'You're looking for a goat!'

They nodded.

'And you think he might have trespassed in my

garden. Again?' The pause before the word 'again' sounded very threatening.

'Oh, no!' Mandy said hastily. 'I'm sure he hasn't!'

'Of course not,' James added. They shifted uncomfortably, managing to get the handlebars of their bikes messily entwined.

Mr Western made a great show of going back through the gates and peering all round his perfect garden. 'No, no goat in here,' he reported cheerfully.

'Why's he being so nice?' James whispered behind his back.

'I don't know, but I don't trust him.' Mandy felt very suspicious. Why wasn't he hysterical with worry about his flower-beds?

'So!' Mr Western came back and faced them, rocking back on his brown leather heels. 'No problem!'

'No . . .' they agreed slowly.

'Well, is there?' He looked sharply at their embarrassed faces.

'Mr Western! Mr Western!' Dennis Saville, the estate manager, suddenly appeared at a run, coming down the side path from the great house. By now light snowflakes were twirling in the gloom, and Dennis held his anorak tight to his throat. He kept calling in a loud voice, 'It's OK, sir! Everything's taken care of!' He came quickly down the main drive towards the gate.

'Very good, Dennis!' Mr Western said stiffly.

'Just like you said. It seems to be working, sir!'

Western cleared his throat, nodding his head towards Mandy and James. 'That's quite right, Dennis. But we've got visitors. I'll come and deal with it soon.'

Then Dennis saw them, and his mouth shut like a clamp. He gave his boss an uncomfortable look.

'These two are looking for a goat,' Mr Western explained. 'You haven't seen one, have you, Dennis?'

'No, sir!' he said like a sergeant-major standing to attention.

'See?' Mr Western nodded and smiled. 'Your goat isn't here. He must be halfway down to Welford by now. I should get a move on.' He closed the gates on the inside. 'Matter of fact, I did hear a bit of a kerfuffle from next door a little while ago. Mrs Parker Smythe was out on her driveway, making some kind of fuss or other shooing something off. Why don't you go and check there?'

Mandy's head was up. She'd recovered from her embarrassment, and every bit of her was alert. Something was going on here! 'Come on!' she said to James. The snow had begun to fall thickly now. 'Or we'll lose Houdini's trail!'

James stood a second or two longer, watching the men trudge back up towards the house. 'You sure?' he asked.

'Shh!' She made a great show of getting on her bike and pedalling off.

'I don't trust them as far as I could throw them!' James said, working hard to catch her up.

'Me neither.' Mandy cycled until they reached the far end of the hedge, but she stopped short of the Parker Smythes' house. 'In fact, I'm really worried!' She looked anxiously at him. Houdini's footprints had come to a dead end. And she was pretty sure that Mr Western had been lying.

James nodded. 'What was Dennis Whatsisname up to before he came running over? What was he going on about?'

'Do you think it was something to do with Houdini?' Mandy asked.

James nodded again.

'Do you think we should find out?'

'Definitely!' he said. 'Come on, let's try getting down this side track.' He abandoned his bike and crept ahead, skirting the edge of Mr Western's garden.

Mandy followed, her heart in her mouth. Sheltered from the snow by the bare but massive beech hedge, they made good progress towards a small side gate which led into a bare concrete courtyard at the back of the house, flanked by smart new barns. 'No Entrance', it said on the gate.

Mandy looked at James, but she was certain of what they had to do. 'Come on,' she said, taking a deep breath.

But the gate was locked. Quietly and quickly they went back to examine the hedge for a gap just wide enough to squeeze through. Sure enough they found one. 'Careful!' James warned. 'There may be dogs!'

But there was worse. Mr Western and Dennis were striding into the yard from the opposite direction and they were heading towards what looked like a dark bundle in the corner. The snow made it difficult to make anything out properly, and Mandy and James had to duck out of sight back into the hedge bottom.

The men stood over the dark shape, prodded it with their feet, muttered and looked up at the sky.

'At least a couple of hours yet,' Dennis said.

Mandy and James watched as the two men backed off the way they'd come, checking the yard as they went.

'Oh, no!' Mandy cried. She felt sick. Suddenly everything fell into place.

'What!' James jumped up to stop her, but Mandy was already up and running towards the still, dark shape in the far corner of the yard. 'Mandy, come back!' he cried.

She didn't listen. She didn't care. She knew it was Houdini. Her worst nightmare was coming true. She arrived at the dark shape and bent over it. It was Houdini!

James followed her and helped her brush the snow away. Mandy knelt on the ground to cradle the poor goat's head. He lay, legs stiff and straight, eyes rolling helplessly. 'What's happening?' James asked, horrified.

Mandy seized at a branch lying close against the wall. 'This!' She closed her eyes in sheer panic. The branch had been torn clean off its bush and some of the newest, tenderest leaves were chewed. 'Rhododendron!' she moaned.

'What's wrong? What's happening?' James said. Green slime was oozing from Houdini's mouth and nose. He could hardly move.

'Poisoned!' Mandy tried to ease the goat's mouth open. 'It's the worst thing they can get hold of. It says so in Dad's book! We've got to do something quick!'

'Where'd he get it? Look!' James grabbed the branch. 'Someone gave it to him on purpose, look!' He showed the raw, torn end of the branch. 'Someone's tried to kill him!'

'Never mind now. We've got to move him!' Mandy gathered all the strength she possessed in her thin frame. 'I'll take his head, you support his back end. Let's get him on his feet!'

They worked together. The goat bawled and

protested, but he stood at last — shaky, head down, but able to stagger.

'Come on, boy, come on!' Mandy eased him forward. 'We've got to get him out of here before those two come back!'

'They'd better not show their faces,' James said, fighting back angry tears. Houdini was in a terrible state, too feeble to do anything but totter forward. 'He won't die, will he?'

Mandy shot him a desperate look. 'Of course not!' she said. 'Just help to move his legs for him. Come on, Houdini, come on, boy!'

They made slow progress, trailing across the new layer of snow towards the 'No Entrance' gate. Breathless with fear, Mandy told James to unbolt it while she cradled Houdini's head and tried once more to clear his mouth and nose.

'Hey!' A terrific shout came from behind. 'You two again! You're trespassing!' Mr Western yelled.

They were within a few metres of safety, James was struggling with the gate, but Mr Western was on their trail, reappearing with a couple of squat, fearsome bulldogs. He lost no time in unleashing them.

'Lift him!' Mandy gasped.

They slung their arms under Houdini's swollen belly. The dogs snarled and barked. They rushed forward, thundering across the yard.

'Hurry!' Mandy fancied she could feel the dog's breath. Just in time, they lifted, staggered and slammed the gate in the dogs' faces. They were off Mr Western's property. He could shout all he wanted, but he couldn't chase them now.

'What next?' James looked wildly up and down the white, deserted lane. He looked desperately at Houdini who was standing again, four-square but shaky, his head down, bawling pitifully.

Mandy took handfuls of snow to clean his face, but still the green slime oozed out. She felt the tears hot on her own cheeks as she stood up straight. 'You wait here,' she told James. She could see the 'Private. No Admittance' sign on the gate at Beacon House. Mrs Parker Smythe wasn't the best bet in the world, Mandy knew. She was rich, but not keen on animals. She thought that money and not love was all that was needed to take care of them, and Mandy had once refused the offer of a home for a kitten there. But still it was all they had by way of help right now. 'I'll go and ask!' she said.

And she fled down the lane. No chance this time of poor Houdini scampering back home, and every minute was vital. She pressed hard on the Parker Smythes' bell, over and over. *Let them be in!* she prayed. *Please let them be in!*

Four

'Who's there?' a woman's voice said through a tinny-sounding intercom. 'I can see you on the surveillance camera, but I don't know who you are.'

'It's Mandy Hope, the vets' daughter. I came to see you when Imogen wanted a kitten once, remember?' Mandy stood in the snow outside the locked gates.

'Ah yes!' Mrs Parker Smythe did remember. 'Just a moment!'

The gates swung open, Mandy raced up the drive, arriving at the front door just as it opened. 'Oh, please, can I use your phone?' she gasped. She was shivering with fear and cold.

'Come in,' Mrs Parker Smythe said stiffly. She

looked down at Mandy's wet boots, up at the snow melting rapidly on her jacket and blonde hair. 'Would you just stand there a moment?' She dashed off and came back with a pile of newspapers which she spread on the immaculate hall tiles. 'Would you step on there please?'

Mandy did as she was told.

'Now!' Mrs Parker Smythe put her manicured hands on her slim hips. Little gold embroidered flowers sparkled on her black mohair jumper. Pink lipstick outlined her worried mouth. 'What is it that you want?'

Mandy dripped on to the newspaper. 'To use your phone! We've got a very sick goat outside. He's been poisoned. I need to ring Animal Ark. It's very urgent!'

'A goat?' Mrs Parker Smythe said cautiously. She peered out of the window into the snow-covered garden. 'Not in the garden I hope?'

'No, he's outside in the lane with my friend! Oh, please!' she said. 'I have to ring for help.' The minutes ticked by. How much of the deadly rhododendron bush had Houdini eaten? And how long ago?

'But it's only a goat, you say?' Mrs Parker Smythe tucked a stray strand of very blonde hair back into place. 'And it's outside in the lane?'

'Only!' Mandy was speechless. Poor Houdini might die!

Again Mrs Parker Smythe studied Mandy's messy boots. 'Ah!' she said, hitting on a solution. 'Of course! Just wait here!'

'Please hurry!' Mandy begged.

'Luckily Imogen's not here today.' The woman paused again at the door into a sitting-room. 'If she'd been here she would have been so upset! Imogen's a very sensitive child!' Then she vanished into the room.

Talk about upset! Mandy thought angrily. Animals could die while human beings got upset! But she was relieved nevertheless when Mrs Parker Smythe came

trotting back in her little gold slippers, carrying a
cordless phone.

'Here!' She held it out at arm's length.

Mandy grabbed it and punched in the numbers.
The phone rang only twice before Jean Knox, the
receptionist, answered.

'Jean, hello, it's Mandy. Is my mum on duty? Can
I speak to her, please?'

Jean said yes straight away, then there was another
short pause before Mrs Hope came to the phone.

'Hello, Mum. We've got an emergency. James and
I are up near the Beacon. Houdini's very sick. Lydia's
goat. Can you come up and fetch us? We have to get
him down to the surgery, it's urgent . . . Yes, we're
just outside Beacon House. We'll wait there!'

'OK,' Mrs Hope said. 'I'll be five minutes.'
Nothing else. The phone went dead. Mandy handed it
back to Mrs Parker Smythe.

She thanked her quickly. 'I have to go. James will
need me to help. Thanks!' She opened the door and
stepped back outside. 'Sorry about the mess!' And she
fled down the drive, scarf and jacket flapping in the
wind. At least the snow had stopped.

James stood huddled next to Houdini. The goat's
weak bawling had grown fainter. He swayed from side
to side while James struggled to keep him upright, and
his head was low.

'It's OK! My mum's on her way up,' Mandy said. 'Is his head down like that all the time?'

'Yes, and his eyes are rolling! I hope she hurries up!'

Five minutes seemed like for ever, but at last the four-wheel drive from Animal Ark came into sight, crawling like a squat, dark beetle up the narrow white lane.

Mrs Hope pulled up and jumped straight out. She glanced at Houdini, then positioned Mandy and James and said, 'Lift!' Within seconds they had the goat in the four-wheel drive and were roaring back down the hill.

'It's bad, isn't it?' Mandy said. She'd stayed in the back with Houdini.

Mrs Hope didn't turn round. 'It looks it. What did he eat?'

'Rhododendron leaves,' James said.

Mrs Hope clamped her mouth shut for a second and shook her head. 'Well, your father's on his way back to the Ark. Jean phoned him to say there was an emergency. We'll have to wait and see what he says.'

They arrived back at the same time as Mandy's father. Everyone scrambled around the back of the vehicle to lift Houdini carefully into the surgery. Simon, the nurse, came running out. Mandy and

James held all the doors open. Now they would know what to do; Simon and her mum and dad.

In the white, hygienic space of the treatment room they set Houdini on a table to examine him. Quietly Mrs Hope explained to her husband. Mandy saw his eyebrows gather in a knot. He stopped palpating the goat's abdomen and stood up straight.

'What?' Mandy cried out. 'What's wrong?'

Mr Hope sighed. 'You're sure it was rhododendron?'

James and Mandy both nodded.

'As far as I know there's no antidote.'

No antidote? What did he mean?

'There's nothing we can do,' he said, stepping back, going over the sink to wash his hands. 'Nothing can cure a goat when it eats this kind of leaf. It's fatal.'

Mandy felt her heart lurch and miss its beat. Her dad was saying Houdini was going to die. There was no help for it.

Mrs Hope came towards Mandy. Her red hair had fallen free and swept across her face. She tried to hug her daughter. 'I'm so sorry!' she said.

But Mandy sprang away.

Houdini kept his eyes on her; he was waiting for her to help. It wasn't true! There must be something they could do! 'Dad!' she cried.

'There's no known antidote, I'm sure of it,' he

repeated. 'I'm sorry, love.' He turned on the tap.

She ran from the room. 'Wait!' she told them.

'Mandy!' her mum called.

Mandy ignored her and rushed to the house, into the kitchen. She seized her dad's college book and sprinted back to the surgery.

'I think it might be best if you didn't go back in,' Jean said from behind her desk.

But Mandy rushed on. 'Wait, wait!' They were lifting Houdini off the table and he was protesting feebly. She found the page in the book. Poisons: yew, laburnum, rhubarb, foxglove . . . rhododendron! 'No antidote. Usually fatal.'

Her heart crashed. Frantically she read on. 'Old countryman's remedy: dissolve bicarbonate of soda into melted lard . . .'

'Look at this!' she shouted.

Mr Hope read over her shoulder and pointed to the line below. 'But look at this,' he said gently. ' "Now discredited. No basis in medical fact, unorthodox and probably ineffective remedy." ' He took the book away. 'It won't work, Mandy. There's no cure for the old chap. I'm afraid you've got to face it.'

Houdini bleated as they carried him out.

'Let me try!' Mandy pleaded. 'At least let James and me try!'

Mrs Hope stepped forward and looked at her

husband and Simon. There was a terrible pause as they considered the situation, then all three nodded. Mr Hope took a deep breath.

'OK, we'll try!'

'Yes!' Mandy and James went rushing to the kitchen for ingredients.

Even Jean, hearing all the noise, left her reception desk to help them melt the lard and dissolve the bicarb.

'It stinks!' James said.

'It's meant to make him sick!' Mandy said. 'He's got to take it over and over until his stomach's empty! It says so in the book!' She'd read every last word of the country remedy and got it by heart.

They went back and dosed the poor animal. Mr Hope supervised as they inserted a tube down Houdini's throat.

'It seems as if it might be working,' he said cautiously after the third dose. 'At least it's doing what they say it's supposed to.'

Mandy read one last sentence from the book. 'It says that when the slimy stuff stops, we stop the bicarb and then dose him with coffee!' she said.

'Coffee!' James, with his sleeves rolled up and a look of concentration on his face, stopped work.

'It's a stimulant,' Mr Hope explained. 'Go on, James. You go and make it good and strong!' He turned to Mandy. 'Once his stomach's clear of this stuff, we'll try the stimulant.'

Still they worked on, taking turns to pour the lard and bicarb mixture down the tube into Houdini's throat, only pausing for him to be sick. A couple of hours had gone by; Houdini was still on his feet, and his mouth and nose were almost clear. 'I'd never have believed it!' Mr Hope murmured. 'He looked like a goner to me!'

Mandy patted Houdini. 'Good boy!' She fed the coffee into his mouth through a new, clean tube. Houdini gulped at the bitter taste. Across the table she could see James nodding and encouraging him to swallow. If willpower alone could keep an animal alive, James and Mandy together would make it happen.

Mr Hope eased open Houdini's powerful jaws to investigate. Then with his stethoscope he went and listened to his heartbeat. 'We're not out of the woods yet,' he said quietly. 'Maybe we should consider a more orthodox stimulant?'

He conferred with Simon then turned back to Mandy. 'Anyway, better not phone Lydia with any premature good news just yet,' he said. He stood back and studied Houdini, whose head was still down.

'She doesn't have a phone,' Mandy reminded him. Then a thought struck her. 'Lydia — she doesn't even know! I'd better go up there and tell her!'

James was still feeding Houdini coffee through the tube. He nodded. 'I'll stay here.'

And hard as it was to leave them, it was harder still thinking of Lydia going about her chores, not knowing that Houdini's life was in danger. Mandy grabbed her coat.

Mr Hope nodded too. 'Simon will drive you up, won't you? Don't worry, we'll take care of things here!'

'I'll see if I can get her to come down.' Mandy took one last look at them all gathered around Houdini, giving the best expert care. Then before she had time to think too hard, she was in Simon's battered old van, careering up the hill towards High Cross.

Lydia stood at the door and listened. She took the news quietly. 'Yes,' she said, 'I understand.' She nodded. 'And is he in a very bad way?

'Yes,' Mandy told her. 'Houdini got hold of the branch in Mr Western's garden. That's where we found him!'

Lydia stared out at the snowy yard, but she didn't look at Mandy. 'We'll have to keep our fingers crossed,' she said.

'Come down with us to Animal Ark. You can help. You must have done this before; you know what to do better than us!' Mandy grabbed her by the arm. Beneath Lydia's calm acceptance of the news, she could see how upset she was.

Lydia considered. 'You've dosed him with the lard and bicarb, you say?' she asked Simon.

Simon nodded.

'And he's been sick? How much of the leaf had he chewed?'

'We don't know.'

'Well, it all depends on how much.' She looked up at the grey snow clouds. 'You've done your best.'

'But will it work?' Mandy asked.

At last Lydia looked directly at her. 'I had six goats get at some rhododendrons once. Oh, it was years ago. I gave them the cure my father would have used, and his father before him, and so on back in time. The same cure you've given Houdini.'

'Well?' Mandy couldn't bear the silences.

'Four lived. Two died.' She stepped back inside the house. It seemed to be her final word.

Mandy looked round at Simon. 'I don't think she'll leave the other goats. She won't come down with us!'

Simon agreed. 'It doesn't look like it.'

'It's not that Lydia doesn't care,' Mandy explained. 'In some ways she cares too much. I think she can hardly bear it, but she knows we've done our best and she just needs some time to face up to it.'

Again Simon nodded.

'You go. I'll stay here!' Mandy said. It was torment not to know whether Houdini was dead or alive, but she felt her place was here now with Lydia.

Simon gave her a brief, sympathetic smile, zipped up his jacket and went back down to the van. 'I'll be back as soon as there's any definite news,' he said.

Inside the kitchen Lydia was calmly making tea. She looked up briefly when Mandy came in. She invited Mandy to sit down by the fire, and carried on. 'You did quite right,' she told her. 'It's a long time since I heard of any modern veterinary being ready to try a country cure like that.'

Mandy raised her eyebrows but kept quiet. The warmth of the fire was beginning to seep through. Somehow Lydia's praise made her want to cry again.

Lydia handed her a cup of tea. 'Now all we can do is wait and see.' She settled herself in another chair opposite. 'Houdini's as strong as the devil!' she said to herself as much as to Mandy.

Mandy sat and watched. Lydia had fallen silent; thinking, thinking.

'Of course,' she said, 'without Houdini I can't carry on here.' The shadows were deepening, the firelight flickering. Mandy's heart missed a beat. 'Without Houdini there won't be any kids next year to keep the herd going or to sell on. And I need the milk, too.'

Mandy didn't try to interrupt, but again the thought of High Cross without Lydia and the goats was more than she could bear. Tears filled her eyes.

Lydia went on sadly. 'We'd have to shut up. The old place would die.' She looked around with moist eyes. 'It's not for myself that I'd mind so much. Of course, I've memories to let go of. But it's my father I mind for. He always hoped I'd carry on. I'd be letting him down.'

'There was your mother too. What happened to her?' Curiosity got the better of Mandy as she sat in the cosy warmth.

'She died when I was born,' Lydia said. 'So I never knew my mother.'

'Me neither,' Mandy confessed. 'Not my real mother. She died, with my father, in a car crash. I was only a baby. I'm adopted.'

Lydia nodded and took Mandy's hand. The floodgates of memory had opened. 'My father doted on me after we'd lost her. I was everything to him. Me and High Cross. He taught me to read before I ever went to school. He taught me a love of books and a love of animals. I helped him from when I was very tiny; in the fields, in the barn.' She paused. 'I was a very happy child.'

'But you're so cut off!' Mandy said. 'Weren't you lonely?'

'Sometimes. I did go to school, however. And I was healthy. I was loved. What's loneliness compared with that?'

'And you never wanted anything different?' Mandy saw how modern life had passed them by up at High Cross, leaving Lydia and her father behind.

'What could I need?' She looked round as if the kitchen at High Cross was world enough. 'And I never married, of course. You might think that odd?'

Mandy shook her head. Knowing Lydia, no.

'I did go out to dances once or twice. The Institute at Welford used to have very nice dances, I remember!' For a moment, memories drew her attention. She looked dreamily into the fire. Then she shook herself back into the present. 'But mostly I was too busy. And to tell you the truth I don't mix easily. I'm a clumsy soul when it comes to people. Whereas with animals now, I'm perfectly easy!' She beamed.

'Me too!' Mandy agreed.

'With animals it's so simple. You tend their needs. And they in their turn will look after you!' She got up and stirred the fire. 'I wonder how that rogue Houdini is getting on!' Her impatience broke through after all in a restless looking out of the window. Then she studied the ancient wooden clock on the mantelpiece. It said a quarter to five. She turned to Mandy. 'I've had many a long hard winter here, and many a long vigil. I only hope this isn't my last!'

And so they paced the kitchen floor together, waiting, waiting.

'Time to go and milk!' Lydia said at last. 'Before dusk.' She pulled on her old brown jacket, shoved her feet into the wellingtons by the door. This was how she kept going, Mandy thought — by doing practical jobs and keeping the animals in perfect order.

But an engine was whining up the hill. Mandy recognised it. The van swung off the road up the final stretch of track to High Cross. Mandy and Lydia ran out through the snow down to the gate to meet it.

Simon slammed on the brakes, slewed sideways and killed the engine. He jumped down from the driver's seat and strode the last few metres up the hill towards them.

Five

Time froze. Seconds seemed to last for ever. Mandy looked into Simon's thin, pinched face for an answer.

'Well?' Lydia said, very brusque.

'He's fine!' Simon said, breaking into a broad grin. 'He's going to be OK!'

Mandy jumped in the air. She whirled round in the snow. She hugged Simon.

'Right,' Lydia said, feet still on the ground. 'There's that milking to do.' But before she walked briskly back up the slope, she allowed herself one fleeting smile and a sigh of relief. 'You might say that was Houdini's greatest escape!' she said.

Mandy and Simon looked hard at each other and laughed.

'No, I truly am pleased!' Lydia told Mandy. 'And I'm very grateful to you for acting so swiftly. I couldn't have done it better myself!' She smiled then walked quickly on.

Mandy glowed under Lydia's praise.

'Is she always this brisk?' Simon nudged Mandy and pointed to Lydia's back.

'She doesn't like strangers.' For a second Mandy was thoughtful. 'Anyway, she's probably worried about Dad's bill.'

She decided to stay on and help Lydia with the milking, and Simon agreed to wait until she was finished. They walked on up after Lydia.

'How long will Houdini need to stay on at our place?' Mandy asked.

'Just overnight,' Simon said. 'We need to check his heart rate in case this bout of poisoning has weakened the heart. It puts a great strain on the old ticker. But your dad's ninety-nine percent sure that everything's OK. He can come back home tomorrow, all being well!'

Still scarcely able to believe it, Mandy set to in the barn, filling the goats' pails with fresh water and mucking out the pens while Lydia led each goat off for milking. 'Come on, Jemima! Whoa, lazy beast!'

Lydia chuntered softly, while the goats nudged against her or reached up for stray mouthfuls of hay. 'There's a good girl, Alexandra, steady girl!' Soon they'd worked their way down each side of the barn and all the goats were milked.

Simon helped out too, carting manure out to the half-frozen heap across the yard. He rolled up his sleeves and whistled cheerfully, telling Mandy a joke every now and then. In an hour they were finished and the goats locked up for the night.

'Nearly dusk,' Lydia said as she locked the barn. She looked up at the sky and allowed herself another sigh. 'The sky's cleared. No doubt it'll freeze tonight.' Then she made a little clearing sound in her throat and nodded at Mandy. 'And tomorrow you'll bring Houdini back home?'

'Yes. Early. Then everything's back to normal.'

'Thanks to you,' Lydia said shyly. Then her face broadened into its lovely smile. 'Tomorrow the thaw will come!'

Mandy looked up at the crystal clear sky. 'How do you know?'

'It's in my bones. Spring is just round the corner, you'll see!' Still smiling, she waved and disappeared into the house.

An idea dawned some time between Mandy's

exhausted head finally hitting the pillow that night and the sun striking her full in the face next morning. It was one of the best ideas she'd ever had. It made her jump out of bed, throw on some jeans and a jumper, dash downstairs, excuse herself from breakfast and morning chores in Animal Ark, and head for James's house almost without pausing for breath.

'Is James in?' she asked Mrs Hunter, just on her way down the drive to take Blackie for his morning walk.

'He's still in bed I think.' Mrs Hunter didn't have time to ask Mandy what she wanted. 'You're up early!'

'Snow's melting!' Mandy yelled. 'Lydia was right!'

Mrs Hunter just shook her head in bewilderment and walked on.

'James!' Mandy rushed into the house and shouted from the bottom of the stairs. 'Get up. I've got an idea!'

'Sounds serious!' Mr Hunter said, emerging from the kitchen, newspaper in hand. 'I should stay out of the way if I were you, James!' he shouted upstairs. 'Mandy's got that look on her face!'

She ignored him. 'James, get a move on!' She watched the little black and white cat, Eric, pad softly downstairs and stooped to say hello. Then James himself appeared, tousled and yawning.

'What time do you call this then?' he grumbled.

'Listen! I've got this really great idea, and you've got to help me make it work!' Mandy said. 'You know Lydia's short of feed up at High Cross? It's even more serious than usual. You know she's really worried about it?'

'Yes,' James said, running his fingers through his messy hair.

'And she can't afford to spend extra money on feeding the herd?'

'Don't tell me. You've thought of a way to help!' James wandered off into the kitchen. 'I don't suppose you've bothered to eat yet?' he checked.

'Do you want to know this plan or not?' she demanded, hands on hips.

'I don't know. Do I want to know this plan, Eric?' James asked the cat.

Eric purred.

'Oh, go on then!' James sighed, putting two slices of bread into the toaster.

'James Hunter, I'll murder you!' But they settled down together at the table, face to face. 'Anyway, are you ready? This is it! It's a plan to help Lydia and the goats! And I think it's one of the most important things we've ever done!'

James listened intently as Mandy explained. Soon his own face lit up. 'Good idea!' he said.

'Do you think it'll work?' She looked eagerly at him. 'And do you know you've got marmalade on your chin?'

He wiped it off. 'Let's try. Just wait while I grab my bike,' he said.

A minute later, zipped inside their warm jackets, they wheeled their bikes to the gate and set off. They met up with Mrs Hunter just as they came out on to Welford's main street, outside the Fox and Goose.

'Wait!' she said, gripping a nearby fence in fake shock. 'Can this be my son James, dressed and out of the house before eight o'clock on a weekend morning?'

'Mum!' he complained. 'We're off to Walton. Is that OK? It's important!'

'It always is.' She winked at Mandy. 'Yes, of course it's OK. But let me give you a word of warning – keep an eye out for Mr Western!'

The name Western pulled them up short again with a squeal of brakes. 'Why? What's he saying?' Mandy asked.

'I saw him in the newsagent's just now, when I called in for my magazine, moaning on about something or other as usual. He'd got a face like thunder. Something about a goat,' Mrs Hope said, arching her eyebrows. 'Now you two wouldn't happen to know anything about a goat in Mr Western's garden, would you? It occurred to me that you might,

James, since you've been spending so much time up at High Cross lately.'

Mandy and James's faces shut down like clamps. 'Murderer!' Mandy said darkly.

'Poisoner!' James echoed.

'What?' Mrs Hunter shook her head. 'Well, he's threatening to get rid of one particular goat once and for all, if he hasn't done it already! I thought I'd better mention it.' She looked quizzically at the two of them. 'Anyway, his car's still outside the shop; I can see it from here. Just in case you want to avoid him!'

'Thanks, Mum!' James nodded and they set off by the side of the church, taking the back road to Walton. By eight-thirty they'd arrived at the supermarket and padlocked their bikes to the rail outside. Early shoppers filled one or two parking spaces, but the shop was still practically deserted. 'Come on!' Mandy said, heading through the automatic doors straight for the manager's office.

The manager was a stout grey-haired man in a neat grey suit. He wore a shiny red badge with the name of his supermarket on it. He had a neat grey moustache, a white shirt and a bright red tie. He listened carefully, nodding every once in a while.

When Mandy and James had finished their request he jotted down one or two details. He glanced at his watch, cleared his throat and picked up the phone.

'I'm calling Head Office,' he explained in a deep, rich voice. Mandy and James sat silently with secretly crossed fingers. Waiting was always agony.

'Hello, Head Office? Gordon Jolly here.'

Mandy rolled her eyes. His name definitely didn't suit him. James stifled a grin.

'Yes. Is that Mr Middleton? Well, sir, I think I've got a good piece of public relations on the go here. There's a couple of youngsters who want us to supply them with some fruit and veg for their pet goat . . . Yes sir, that's right!'

James nudged Mandy, who was about to protest at the word 'pet'. He shook his head. She bit her tongue.

'Fruit and veg past its sell-by date, that's right, sir, you've got it! Yes, they seem a nice pair of kids and we could certainly do with the good publicity. Local kids. Word of mouth kind of thing. ''Supermarket gives away surplus veg for good cause.'' You know the sort of thing? . . . Yes, sir, that's fine! Thank you, sir!' He put the phone down with a neat click. 'Well,' he said, 'there's just one problem.'

'Oh?' Mandy and James's spirits fell.

'Delivery!'

'Oh!' Mandy cheered up instantly. 'That's no problem!'

Mr Jolly looked out of the window. He tapped his pen on the desk. 'Of course, we couldn't possibly

deliver it. The cost . . . well, the cost!' He shrugged his shoulders.

'No, of course not,' said Mandy. 'But we can collect it ourselves each day after school.'

'What in?' Mr Jolly asked, looking for a truck or a van at least.

'On our bikes!' Mandy said.

Only when they were loaded down with cabbages, broccoli, celery and carrots, only when the bright red supermarket bags were safely slung from the handlebars of their bikes and stacked high in panniers did Mr Jolly believe them. 'Well!' he said. 'I certainly admire your spirit!'

'Thank you!' they said, overjoyed.

'Any time. I'll tell my fresh produce manager to put something aside each day!' By now he was smiling broadly and living up to his name.

'Just until we get through this cold snap,' Mandy promised.

'Only too pleased to help!' Mr Jolly said, smiling and waving, standing there in his neat grey suit. 'Only too pleased!'

They rode steadily out of the car park. 'Nice man,' James said. Then, 'Nice idea!'

Mandy blushed. 'Thanks.'

' ''Any time! Only too pleased!'' ' James mimicked the supermarket manager's fruity voice.

Laughing, they pedalled the low road back to Welford. 'I must remember to bring my rucksack in future,' Mandy commented.

'Houdini had better be grateful, that's all I can say!' James gasped.

'Well, let's go and see.' Mandy pulled up in front of Animal Ark. 'It must be just about time for him to go home to High Cross!' she said.

Houdini was in fine fettle as they led him out of the surgery into the four-wheel drive. His intelligent black head was up and he was high-stepping up the ramp into the back of the vehicle. Mandy felt very proud that her cure had worked, against all the odds. She grinned at Houdini.

'Just a second — I left his collar at the desk!' Mrs Hope said.

Jean Knox came back out with her to say goodbye, giving Houdini a scratch on his head, between his horns. He flicked an ear and licked her fingers.

Mrs Hope was fastening his collar when Mandy remembered something. 'Mum . . .' she began.

'What?' Mrs Hope stopped a moment. 'I know that tone of voice, Mandy. It's your "can I ask a favour" tone!'

James, who was trying to keep Houdini separate from the supermarket loot in the front passenger seat, leaned out of the window. 'Get a move on!' he said. 'Please!' Houdini had already nibbled a large hole in one of the carrier bags.

'Well?' Mrs Hope asked with a warm smile. 'Go ahead, shoot!'

'It's about our bill for Houdini's treatment.' Mandy wondered how best to explain, then went for the direct method. 'Well, Lydia can't afford to pay it. I'm sure she can't! She can't even afford extra feed for the goats. That's why she's never been near a vets for years. And our bill would be much more than she could pay, with the call-out and the boarding charge and everything!'

Mrs Hope considered and nodded.

'I wondered if we could make Houdini's treatment free this time? Just this once!' Mandy knew her mum was pretty tough about these things. After all, she had a business to run. 'I'm really worried about Lydia. Honestly, Mum!'

Mrs Hope kept on nodding gently. 'Well,' she said, 'this question of the fee for treating Houdini – I would have said that in this case it's very much up to the particular vet in the practice who treated him!'

'Dad?' Mandy said, looking round hopefully to see if she could spot him.

'Come on!' James yelled again from inside the car, getting desperate. 'Back, Houdini! Get back!'

'No, not your dad,' Mrs Hope said. She tucked her scarf up under her chin. 'You!'

'Me?'

'Yes, you're the one who diagnosed Houdini's problem and brought him in. You're the one who said he was worth treating when we'd already given up. And you're the one who decided on the course of treatment. Yes, I should definitely say you were the vet in charge there!'

Mandy beamed and her eyes shone. 'Great!' she said. 'So I say there's going to be no charge!'

They clambered into the four-wheel drive together. 'You'll never get rich, Mandy Hope!' her mum said, smiling.

No, but I'll be happy, she thought, hugging Houdini tight round the neck.

And Lydia had been right about the thaw. The sun had got up strong and bright by the time they reached High Cross, and the snow was slipping in great wet sheets from the roofs of the house and barns, landing with wet thuds on the cobbled yard.

Lydia heard the car and came out to greet Houdini, arms open, smiling her broad smile. 'Well, Houdini! Well, my lad!'

She showered him with affection. Houdini repaid her with little skips of delight across the cobbles, going hard at people's pockets for treats.

'Fit as a fiddle!' Lydia said admiringly. 'And already up to your old tricks!'

Mrs Hope smiled. 'Well, I have some calls to make and must be on my way,' she said. She shook hands politely and shook her head when Lydia struggled through blushes to mention what she must owe.

'Talk to my daughter about it,' Mrs Hope said. She left James and Mandy with Lydia, all making much of Houdini, who lapped up the attention. 'Oh!' she called from the car, 'what about all these carrier bags?'

So they unloaded their hoard of vegetables and headed back to the barn.

'Careful!' James said as they struggled with the heavy bags.

'That's the last one,' Mandy said, dumping a bag of carrots inside the barn door.

Lydia stood by in disbelief. With the smell of fresh food in the air, all the goats set up a clatter inside their pens. Lydia kept shaking her head and laughing. 'Are you sure?' she said. 'Is this for us? Well, I never!' as they tipped bruised apples into each feeding pail and a quick black head popped through each hole to snap up the treat.

Mandy fed Houdini straight from her hand, enticing him back into his pen. She closed the bottom half of the door on him before he had time to protest.

'There!' she said, leaning her forearms along the door in total satisfaction. 'Safe and sound!'

Houdini tossed his head and snickered.

Sunlight poured into the barn in a sharp, clear shaft. Lydia and James fed the other goats green cabbage leaves and broccoli from the bags. Outside, on a slope beyond the house, crocus shoots poked through the melting snow. Mandy chose Houdini the choicest cabbage leaf. He took it delicately between his bottom teeth and upper gum, then curled his bottom lip up slowly, luxuriously. The cabbage leaf vanished in an instant.

'Magic!' Mandy laughed.

And Houdini stretched his lips, leaned back and brayed.

'He says thank you,' Lydia explained. 'Thank you very much!'

Six

Mandy was working in the residential unit at Animal Ark on what even she had to admit were the everyday chores. She was cleaning cages and mopping floors, but she kept her mind active with visions of springtime up at High Cross.

For now Mandy had a mission. In their own minds she and James called it 'Save High Cross Farm'. She knew that the supply of fresh fruit and vegetables was only the first step of many. She swore to herself that nothing would get in the way of saving Lydia and the goats from spending another terrible winter like the one just past. And she swore too that Sam Western would never again get Houdini into his clutches!

The goats were now allowed out into a field by day and taken into the barn at night. The sight of the three kids now approaching a year old was a delight. Monty especially was a frisky, agile, naughty little thing. He duelled with his hornless head and danced up close whenever anyone went near with a carrot or an apple from the supermarket supply.

Lydia was forever hammering new stakes into the hard earth to make fenceposts for the wire netting, but the young goat was forever finding new ways of defeating her. He seemed to have a magic sixth sense for a weak spot in a fence, and he would charge at it, head down, until he battered it low enough to climb over. Then Lydia would be out in the lane after him, talking and coaxing him back into the field with a choice stick of celery before he had time to hightail it down to the Hall. She had to have eyes in the back of her head.

'A penny for your thoughts?' Mr Hope asked. He'd taken his white coat down from the peg, ready to begin morning surgery.

'They're not worth it,' said Mandy. 'I'm just daydreaming.'

He smiled. 'Why don't you go off and get a bit of fresh air? I'll get Simon to finish here.'

But Mandy didn't like to give up on a job. She

fetched the mop and poured disinfectant into the bucket of steaming water. 'What would make an ideal fence to keep goats secure, Dad?' She swished the polished floor with water, one section at a time.

'Ah, goats!' Mr Hope took a miserable-looking hamster from its cage and gently turned it face up on the palm of his hand. He examined its abdomen for swelling. 'I might have known.' There was another long pause. 'Chain link, I suppose.'

'What's that?'

'The sort of thing they use to keep football fans off the pitch. Or they use it around tennis courts. It's tough, and it lasts.' He put the hamster gently back in her cage. 'Even Houdini couldn't escape from a field fenced with that!'

'It would have to be high.'

'Three metres or so.'

'Is it expensive?'

Mr Hope nodded. 'Too dear for Lydia, if that's what you're thinking.'

Mandy admitted it. She stood up straight and ran one hand through her short blonde hair, making it stand up at different angles. 'I'm worried about Mr Western. He keeps telling people that Lydia's goats have ruined his garden. It's not even true! Houdini might have paid him a couple of visits, but you can't call that "ruined"!'

'I agree,' Mr Hope said. 'There's no need to get excited.'

But there was. 'He just tried to do away with Houdini with that terrible rhododendron branch. He made Dennis Saville feed it to Houdini, I know he did! And next time they'll manage it!'

Mandy resumed mopping the floor, savagely now. 'We've got to keep Houdini away from there. And the young ones. There's one called Monty who's nearly as good at escaping as Houdini!'

Mr Hope listened as he worked. 'You'll think of something,' he said. 'You always do!'

'What we need is good strong fencing around the small top meadow, and someone to fix it!'

In fact, finding the fencing for the meadow proved very difficult indeed. Mandy rang garden centres and builders all around Welford and Walton, checking prices. *You'd need to be a millionaire!* she thought. She put down the phone and finally gave in. It was just too expensive to consider.

The date of the spring show, a high point in the Welford year, was rapidly approaching. Her father was getting pretty fit for the fell race, but still Mandy thought she might drag him out on another training run, to try and take her mind off fences. They took the normal route out of Welford up towards the Beacon.

'Keep going, Dad! Six minutes thirty seconds!' Mandy encouraged, shouting from her bicycle. They drew level with the dreaded Upper Welford Hall. The garden preened itself in the spring sunshine. Thousands of daffodils waved in the breeze like a golden sea. Green shoots sprouted on the hedges.

Mr Hope willed himself to the top of the hill. But Beacon House was his limit. He collapsed on a grassy bank outside the gates. 'Give me five minutes!' he gasped.

So Mandy left her bike and strolled off, still thinking *Lydia — fencing — goats — Lydia,* like a chant inside her head. She couldn't get rid of the problem of the fencing.

And it appeared, like magic, as if she'd willed it. There, inside the vast garden of Beacon House, was the Parker Smythe tennis-court. And there, by brilliant coincidence, was just the fence! Two workmen, busy resurfacing the court with an expensive all-weather surface, had dismantled the old chain link fence. It lay in giant rolls beside brand-new shiny rolls of the stuff. Mandy stood dumbstruck, her mind in a whirl.

'Hi!' she shouted to the workmen. They stopped work and strolled over. 'What are you going to do with all that old wire fencing?'

One man scratched his chin. The other man opened a can of Coke and drank great swigs. 'Scrap it,' the first one answered. 'Why?'

Mandy's heart raced. As usual she came straight to the point. 'Could I have it, please?'

The corners of his mouth went down and he shrugged. 'It's not ours to give.'

'Anyway, how would you shift it?' the other man asked.

Mandy hadn't thought of that.

'You'd need a truck the size of ours at least.' The second, younger, man walked off, unwilling to waste any more time. But the older man with dark, wavy hair, a big nose and a red face, stood and considered the problem.

'Supposing you could shift it — what's it for?' he asked.

'To keep goats fenced in.' Mandy leapt at the chance to explain. She told him about Houdini and young Monty.

'Good idea,' he agreed. 'This would be just the right stuff.' But he scratched his stubbly chin again. 'The missus is out at the moment. She's the one to ask. She's the boss.'

Mandy knew this was true. Mrs Parker Smythe ran the place like an empress, in her golden slippers and bracelets.

'Come back later,' the man suggested. 'There's no harm in asking!'

Mandy nodded. She needed a bit of time to plan. Her dad was up on his feet, limbering up for phase two of his jog. 'What time will she be back?'

'Well, she went off to collect the little girl from riding. I don't expect she'll be long.'

Mandy thanked him and sprinted back to her father.

'You look pleased with yourself!' Mr Hope said, back in his stride alongside Mandy's bike.

'Yup!' she grinned.

Fate meant her to have that fence!

'You'd need someone to put it up,' James pointed out. They'd met up in McFarlane's post office, buying crisps.

She sighed. 'Why does everyone always have to be so practical? First of all the workman says I'll need a lorry to carry it. Secondly you tell me I'll need someone to fix it in place! Why don't you say, "Brilliant! Great! Let's go for it!"?'

'Because you *do* need someone to do the work,' James persisted. 'It's logical.'

They walked out on to the high street, munching crisps.

Mandy sighed, but he was right. They couldn't manage this themselves. They crossed the courtyard in front of the Fox and Goose. 'But we can't just drop the idea because there are a few problems!' she protested.

'It's a good idea, that's for sure.' James walked alongside. 'But who do we know who can put up fences?'

'And who has the time?'

'Who knows Lydia well enough to want to help?'

'No one,' Mandy admitted. They wove through the parked cars in the pub carpark, slowing their pace as the problems of the fence seemed to grow. Still, Mandy refused to be put off. When there were animals in need she never gave in.

'Hello there,' said a deep voice, stopping them in their tracks.

'Ernie!' they said in chorus. Ernie Bell was a stubborn old man who loved animals, though he didn't like to show it. He and Mandy were firm friends.

'How's the kitten?' Mandy said.

'How's Sammy?' James added. Sammy was an orphan squirrel adopted by Ernie.

'Grand!' Ernie said with a smile. He beckoned them over to the little terrace of cottages beyond the carpark. 'Come over and have a look.' He took pleasure in showing them a sleek, proud Tiddles and a chatterbox squirrel scampering in his purpose-built run in the back garden.

Mandy always took a special interest in Tiddles. She bent to stroke her. The cat wound herself around Mandy's ankles.

'That's a great run you built for Sammy!' James said in a very loud, slow voice.

Mandy's mouth fell open.

'I mean, you must be pretty good with wood and wire netting and stuff to build something as strong as that!' James continued. He gave Mandy a long and significant look.

'Ought to be,' Ernie said, gruff but flattered. 'I used to be a carpenter once upon a time. Ran my own little business.'

'But you kept your tools and things?' James bent to

tickle Sammy's nose through the netting. 'He's very friendly,' he said with a grin.

'Cupboard-love,' Ernie grumbled. 'Here, give him a peanut!' He handed a few nuts to James and watched his squirrel take the treat.

'Ernie!' Mandy said brightly. She took over from James. *What a brilliant idea!* she thought. 'I bet you're the best carpenter for miles!'

Ernie blew out his cheeks and gave a little 'huh' sound. 'Flattery!' he said scornfully. 'What's behind it?'

'Ernie!' she said again, sounding shocked this time. 'It happens to be true. Why should anything be behind it?'

'Aye, but it is,' Ernie said flatly. 'I know when there's a favour in the air.'

Mandy sighed. 'Oh, well, if you don't want to help . . .'

She knew from experience that Ernie would always do the opposite of whatever you expected him to do.

'I never said that!' he protested. He looked sideways at Mandy. 'I never said I wouldn't help!'

'Oh, but you wouldn't want to be bothered. It's a long way out of the village, up by the Beacon. It'd be too much trouble.'

Ernie stood in his little scrap of garden, feet wide apart, hands in his trouser pockets. 'Who says it'd be too much trouble?' He looked stubborn and grumpy.

'Oh, it's just Lydia Fawcett up at High Cross, that's all.' Mandy risked a quick glance at James. He was nodding in support.

'I know the place,' Ernie said. 'Old Frank Fawcett ran a tidy farm, but he was a touch old-fashioned, I hear. Not a regular down in the village.'

'I know. And his daughter's just the same. She's probably not your sort either. She keeps herself to herself.' Mandy crossed her fingers behind her back.

'Oh, I don't mind that,' Ernie objected. 'I'm the sort to mind my own business too.'

Mandy nodded, then she took a deep breath. 'She just needs a new fence, that's all. But I'm sure you wouldn't be interested.'

'New fence?'

'Oh, it'd be ever so much work,' she said. 'Wouldn't it, James? I expect it would be more than one person could handle anyway. And she's got no money to pay for the work!'

James agreed. 'No, we shouldn't have said anything.'

'Right!' Ernie snapped his fingers. 'If she wants a fence, tell her I'm her man!'

'Oh, no, Ernie!' they protested.

'Yep. I can do with the fresh air and exercise,' he said, heading indoors. 'And I like a bit of a challenge, else I get rusty. When does she want me to start?'

'Tomorrow!' Mandy said, swallowing hard. Sometimes you had to take a risk.

'Eight o'clock sharp,' Ernie said.

'It's Sunday tomorrow,' James pointed out.

'Aye, eight o'clock on Sundays. Otherwise it'd be seven!' And Ernie closed the door firmly in their faces.

Mandy and James rode off, delirious with success. 'Now all we have to do is get our fence!' Mandy cried.

'Oh, no, I don't think so!' Mrs Parker Smythe said through thin shiny pink lips. 'That doesn't sound like a good idea at all!'

Mandy's heart sank. But with James standing alongside her she gained a bit more courage. 'Lydia really does need better fencing for the goats. And we thought if you didn't need this old stuff it would still be really useful for her!'

Mrs Parker Smythe stood in the doorway backed by the white marble splendour of her hall. Imogen Parker Smythe peeped out from behind her mother, black riding-hat still strapped firmly on her chubby head. 'I'm afraid that woman is rather a nuisance in the neighbourhood,' she said coolly.

Mandy struggled to bite back a lively defence of Lydia. How could they call her a nuisance? Anger nearly choked her.

'She really can't expect any favours in the circumstances!'

Imogen smirked. Mandy went very red in the face.

'Lydia doesn't even know we're asking,' James explained. 'It was our idea. We just saw the spare fencing ourselves.' But his voice was fading at the set look on Mrs Parker Smythe's face.

'Well, I'm sorry!' she rolled on. 'But I think she may be pulling the wool over your eyes. And you'll understand if I have to say no.'

Mandy bit back her disappointment.

'I'm sure our neighbour, Mr Western, wouldn't thank us for offering charity to the woman on the hill, as he calls her. In fact, he'd probably never speak to us again!' She laughed a high, unfunny laugh and began to close the door on them. 'In any case, my husband isn't here, and we'd need time to discuss this sort of thing with him!'

Just then, Mr Parker Smythe's black sports car entered between the electronic gates and swept up the drive. He gave the workmen a wave and pulled up at the front door. He got out then bent to hug Imogen as she ran out and clambered over him in full riding gear.

'Hello, pet,' he said. And even Imogen looked like a normal, unspoilt child, glad to see her dad. 'Hello?' he said to Mandy and James.

'Oh, darling!' his wife said. 'I was just trying to explain!' She pecked him on the cheek. 'I'm saying we can't just hand on the old fencing from the tennis-court. I mean, it's not as simple as that!'

'Oh?' Mr Parker Smythe looked with renewed interest at Mandy. 'What on earth do you want with our old fencing?'

'To help put up good fencing for the goats at High Cross!' Mandy explained immediately, fired up with defence of Lydia. 'She may not have any money, but she's a good farmer, and she works and works, all by herself up at that farm, with no one to help! She keeps fantastic goats! They're the most beautiful creatures you could imagine, and it's all because of Lydia!'

Mr Parker Smythe frowned. He looked quite frightening in this serious, unsmiling mood. He was the sort who never got excited or involved, Mandy decided. She didn't think he would say 'yes' where his wife had said 'no', but at least she'd had a really good try.

'Sam Western says the woman and her goats are a terrible nuisance! They keep on ruining his flowers!' Mrs Parker Smythe reminded him. 'The neighbourhood would be better off without her and her hideous creatures!' She stood and stared at Mandy, tapping her pink fingernails against the doorpost.

'Hmm.' Mr Parker Smythe looked irritated, but at what? 'Who was here first? That's the question I'd like to ask.'

'Pardon?' Mrs Parker Smythe's voice went high and brittle.

'I mean, I'm sure Lydia Fawcett and her family have been farming at High Cross longer than Sam Western and his fancy machines at the Hall!'

'She has!' Mandy said, utterly amazed.

'Well, Sam Western had better keep quiet about the tone of the neighbourhood and such nonsense,' Mr Parker Smythe said fiercely. His wife began to crumple. 'Listen,' he told her. 'We live here in this beautiful house. But we haven't always had such a good life, you know that!'

He was really annoyed. Then he pulled himself together. 'Look,' he said, 'I've had a long day, I'm sorry!' Mr Parker Smythe walked over to the workmen. 'Break off for half an hour,' he told them. 'Load the old fencing on to the truck and drive it up to the farm, would you? These kids will show you the way.'

Mandy couldn't believe her ears. The friendly workman gave her a thumbs up. 'Thank you!' she gasped. She knew there was no need to say any more.

Mr Parker Smythe nodded and smiled. 'I'm glad to be able to help,' he said. 'Very glad. You can tell

Lydia Fawcett that I'm pleased to be able to help a good neighbour! In fact, tell her I'll call in myself to say so!' And he went inside. He'd said the last word. It was settled.

'Yes!' Mandy and James yelled with delight. They ran over to the truck. Up went the rolls of wire netting, off went the truck along the bumpy lane.

Lydia came to the door with a look of complete surprise.

'Don't say anything!' Mandy warned as they pulled up at the old gate. She was out in the yard in her wellingtons and brown jacket, peering up at the fencing. 'I'll explain later!'

And Lydia watched in disbelief as the men unloaded the great rolls of fencing into her yard.

It took all of next morning to convince her that this was her fence, even though it had been sitting in the yard all night waiting for Ernie Bell.

When he arrived, he measured it and found that it would go right around the small top meadow. It was about two and a half metres high. Ernie explained to Lydia that he was there to trim and drive wooden stakes into the ground. Then he would nail the wire netting to the posts. No goat would ever be able to escape from one of his fences. And it wouldn't cost her a penny!

Mandy's plan was working out perfectly. She went

about all day with a huge smile.

Lydia was speechless. She came out and milked the goats, eyeing Ernie with double suspicion. She tramped silently inside in her wellingtons.

'Not over-friendly, is she?' Ernie commented.

Mandy laughed. 'She is when she gets to know you!' She knew Lydia always made a bad first impression.

'Aye well, it's nothing to me whether or not she's on speaking terms,' Ernie grumbled. He worked neatly and quickly. No one could make a better job of a fence than Ernie Bell!

Lydia came out again to offer a cup of tea.

'Milk and two sugars,' Ernie muttered.

'You'll have to do without saucers,' Lydia said firmly. 'I won't bring my best cups out here to get chipped for anybody!' But Mandy knew she was weakening. Before Ernie left, she might even offer him a smile!

And when the fence was up, tall and straight, Lydia went into the barn to fetch Houdini. He came trotting out, sniffing the fresh air, looking for a chance to escape. But he stopped short. He pawed the grass. Lydia had led him into the middle of the new compound. All around, the fencing towered.

Houdini turned his head full circle. He looked at Lydia. He looked at the fence. He measured his distance, head down, ready to charge.

'Houdini!' Lydia said sternly.

And he thought better of it. The clever goat saw that this fence was like no other. It was unbreakable! So he lifted his head, turned haughtily and strode off to the top end of the meadow. 'Perhaps I'll stay, perhaps I won't!' he seemed to say. He took a delicate nibble of fresh dandelion leaf.

Ernie, Lydia and Mandy stood and watched.

'Well, I reckon we won that battle!' Ernie said.

'But maybe not the war!' Lydia warned as they went out through the tall gate. They left Houdini safely fenced in − for the moment at least.

Seven

'Extra food and a fence — that's not bad going!' Mrs Hope told Mandy. 'As well as saving Houdini's life, of course!'

Mandy felt herself go red. Her plan to save High Cross was going from strength to strength.

It was a warm spring day at last and they were relaxing on the sunny patio at the side of the house. The pink blossom was just beginning to bud on the trees. 'How nice just to sit out in the sun!' Mrs Hope said, curled like a cat in a cream canvas chair.

'Olivia and Lady Jayne are about to kid,' Mandy said, squinting up at the horizon. 'Lydia says it won't be long now before the goats are born.'

'Does that mean you won't be in for lunch?' her mum said, trying to hide a smile. 'What about Gran and Grandad? They're coming over later.'

Mandy stood and paced up and down the patio. 'They won't mind if I'm not here, will they? Just this once?' She looked at her watch. James was due any minute.

'Oh, dear, you're as bad as any father waiting for the birth of a first baby!' Mrs Hope said. 'Can't you sit down?'

'Sorry!' Mandy sat. 'I'm sure everything's going to be fine! Lydia's used to doing this.' She chewed nervously at the end of her thumb. 'Oh, come on, James!' she said.

'Why don't you go on ahead, and I'll tell him to follow?' Mrs Hope suggested. 'But just do one thing for me, dear.'

'What?' Mandy was on her feet quick as a flash, heading for her bike in the garage.

'Just call in at Lilac Cottage to explain. Your gran and grandad will understand, I'm sure!' Anything to do with Mandy and animals took first place, they knew.

Mandy nodded and gave a sheepish grin. 'OK, and tell James to hurry!' She shot off on her bike up the lane, stopping briefly at her grandparents' house.

Grandad was busy in the back garden. He was

mulching his prize leeks, ready for the show. Mandy explained her errand up at High Cross.

'Oh,' he said. 'Goats in kid, eh? Well then!' He stood up and grinned broadly.

'What's this about goats?' Gran came bustling out of the house. 'Who's having a kid? Well then, what are you waiting for? Better get a move on!'

Mandy didn't need telling twice. 'Thanks!' she yelled as James rode up on his bike.

All the way up past Beacon House and Upper Welford Hall she felt convinced they would be late. Olivia and Lady Jayne would have had their kids during the night and they would have missed it.

Mandy had slowed down to a stroll by the time she crossed the yard at High Cross. James scooted up quickly from behind. 'We're too late,' she said to him gloomily. 'I'm sure of it!'

'Quick!' Lydia shot out of the barn towards the house. She didn't stop to say hello. 'Help me get water on to boil. Then fetch some clean straw for bedding! And, James, bring that crate from the corner. That's right. Just take the books out of it! Come on, get a move on!'

They all ran out of the kitchen together. Mandy climbed the ladder to the loft for fresh straw and scrambled down again with great armfuls.

'Shh!' Lydia warned. 'Put the straw in the crate.

Stand back. Give her plenty of room!' They stood outside Olivia's pen, waiting anxiously.

The goat turned and shunted sideways in her pen. She pawed at the stone beneath her straw as if trying to dig. All the time she pushed and barged around in her small space and ignored them.

'She's grinding her teeth,' Lydia pointed out. 'That tells us she's nearly ready!'

'What about the water?' Mandy asked. They'd left two panfuls to heat on the hob.

'With luck we won't need it,' Lydia said. 'She looks to me as if she'll be able to manage.'

It was too much for James. 'I'll go and check the water anyway!' he gulped, and shot out of the barn.

By now Olivia stood straining. And sure enough, two little hooves appeared, with a tip of dark nose, easy to recognise.

Lydia nodded. She went and stood by Olivia's head, encouraging her, whispering, 'Good girl, Olivia, good girl.' The goat pushed again. As the kid eased itself out, Lydia moved round smoothly to take its weight and lower it gently on to the straw. Then she stepped back to allow Olivia to lick the kid clean with her gentle tongue.

Mandy stood by, enthralled.

Quietly Lydia came forward to help clean the kid. She rubbed softly with a towel, paying compliments to

the new mother. 'A fine kid, well done! A little nanny for you, Olivia!' From her pocket she took a tiny brown bottle, placed the corner of the towel against it and poured out a drop or two of strong-smelling liquid. She dabbed the end of the kid's cord with it. 'Iodine,' she explained. 'Now it's time to put her in the crate. Lift her gently.'

Mandy lifted the gangling, kicking creature and put it bleating into the safety of the crate while Lydia went to work, quickly milking an exhausted Olivia. 'Then you can rest,' she told her. 'Don't worry, we'll take care of your little daughter!' And she explained to Mandy that what she was taking from Olivia was colostrum, which they would feed to the kid from a bottle. 'It's full of antibodies to protect the little ones from illness. Then the milk comes!'

Mandy nodded. She was learning so much with the birth of this kid. 'You missed it!' she told James, who had sidled gingerly back into the barn.

'Ah, but we'll need you both this time,' Lydia said, opening the door to Lady Jayne's pen. Her smile had changed to a frown. Lady Jayne was a much smaller goat than Olivia, and this was her first birth. 'She's carrying more than one kid,' Lydia explained. 'And I'm afraid she's struggling.'

James swallowed hard and pushed his glasses further on to his nose.

'OK?' Mandy asked.

He nodded. 'What do I have to do?'

'Fetch the water, quick!' Lydia ordered. She'd taken off her jacket and slung it over the door. 'And bring the disinfectant standing on the sill!'

They ran, fear shooting through them. Something might go badly wrong unless they hurried.

They raced back, balancing the pans of hot water carefully covered with lids. Lydia poured it and some disinfectant into a metal bowl, dipped a cloth into it and talked calmly to Lady Jayne, whose head was down. She was making a dreadful grinding noise with her teeth. 'There, there,' Lydia soothed, 'it'll soon be over!'

She washed the goat's hindquarters, then she scrubbed her own hands and arms. 'You stand by the head!' she told James. 'Keep talking. Tell her it'll be all right!' She nodded at Mandy. 'I'll need you back here. Be ready to take this first kid and clean it up, while I deal with the second!'

Then she soaped one hand thoroughly. 'See, no head showing!' She pointed to the two tiny hooves. Then she took hold of them and pushed hard, so that the kid disappeared completely back into the womb. 'Just a bit of rearranging,' she said, very matter of fact. She felt her way. 'I have to bring the head forward.' And she went on turning the invisible kid into the correct position.

'Good girl!' James stammered. His voice sounded wobbly.

Lydia stood back at last and waited for the hooves to reappear. This time the little point of the nose came with them. They sighed. Now everything went as before. Lydia eased the kid out into the world, handed him to Mandy and let her clean him off. The twin came soon after, easy as anything.

So there were three perfect kids, fluffy and black, with tiny white speckles and stripes to tell one from another. The two mother goats were comfortably bedded down and James recovered enough to come and coo over the babies in the box. Lydia named each one in turn. 'Catherine,' she said. 'And Anne. They were wives of Henry the Eighth, I think.' She considered the male kid for a while. 'Well, why not Henry!' she decided.

They went out beaming into the early afternoon sunshine. 'We'll let the mothers feed them for a few days — after they've had a good rest, that is.' Lydia was rolling down her sleeves and buttoning up her jacket, in spite of the sun. 'Then we'll bottle-feed, and establish Olivia and Lady Jayne in the milking routine.' She was smiling with satisfaction at a job well done.

Mandy slopped the soapy water from the bowl into a drain outside the kitchen door. She took a deep breath of fresh air.

Lydia gave her a tiny, friendly pat on the shoulder. 'How do you like being a midwife?' she asked.

'I love it!' Mandy said, elated. She felt it was the most important thing she'd ever done in her life.

James nodded, but he didn't quite put it into words.

'Well done,' Lydia told him.

The day was made perfect when Mr and Mrs Hope turned up at the gate in their Land-rover. 'We'll go away again if you like!' Mrs Hope called cheerfully. 'We don't want to be in the way!'

'We couldn't keep away,' Mr Hope said sheepishly. 'We wanted to take a look at the kids, if you don't mind, Miss Fawcett?'

Lydia hesitated for half a second, then treated him to one of her gracious, old-fashioned bows. She held one arm towards the barn and said, 'This way please. Follow me.'

Mandy grinned at her mum and dad. They all went in together. Mrs Hope and Lydia bent close together over the tea chest, examining the newly-born kids.

'They're beautiful!' Mrs Hope breathed. 'You did so well!' For Mandy had already told her about the difficult birth.

'Thank you,' Lydia said shyly, accepting the praise.

They all had tea at High Cross, and there were lively voices in the lonely rooms; bright chatter and satisfied smiles.

'And how about the proud father?' Mr Hope asked on the way out. So they went to visit Houdini in the top meadow, complete with fence, where celandines and watercress had come out on the banks of the stream to provide him with choice nibbles. He and Monty grazed peacefully together as the group approached.

Houdini spotted them and graciously came over to say hello.

Mr Hope leaned his weight against a fencepost to test it. 'Pretty good,' he said admiringly.

They'd just started to discuss the pros and cons of

removing the horns from young kids when up the path strode Sam Western with his two dogs!

Houdini saw him first. Down went the head, and he charged straight at the fence with an almighty crash.

Mr Western stopped in his tracks despite the strong, high fence. He called his dogs to heel. 'I say!' he shouted bossily.

Lydia stiffened. She recognised him instantly, though he'd never paid her the honour of a visit before. 'Calm down, Houdini!' She talked gently to the goat until he agreed to trot off down the meadow. 'Now what does he want?' she muttered, straightening her jacket. It was as if a dark cloud had come from nowhere over a perfect sky.

'Need any help?' Mr Hope asked.

Mandy could only glower from a distance. How dare Sam Western come up here after what he'd tried to do to Houdini!

'No, thank you,' Lydia said firmly. She went to open the gate, perfectly civil, and let Sam Western set foot on her land.

'I'd set Houdini on him!' Mandy muttered.

'And he'd have the police on you!' Mrs Hope pointed out. Their little group stood by and watched to see how Lydia would deal with Sam Western.

The audience didn't put him off. 'I've come to give you fair warning!' he said in his loud, confident voice.

He eyed the new fence and her group of friends with some surprise.

'Have you now?' Lydia was still very calm. She only came up as far as Sam Western's shoulder, but she didn't have a scrap of fear in her body.

'Yes. I know my rights in this matter and I won't have your animals tramping all over my property!'

'No,' Lydia agreed. 'It's most unfortunate.'

Western felt the glares from Mandy and the others but this only seemed to make his temper worse. 'There are valuable plants in my garden — show plants. Roses which are almost ready for the spring show. Now I insist that you don't let your goats anywhere near in future!'

Lydia nodded steadily. 'I'll do my best.' She eyed him squarely.

But Sam Western stormed on. 'I'm telling you, if it happens again, I won't answer for the consequences!'

'Then I'll do my best,' Lydia promised.

Sam Western glared at Houdini with concentrated hatred. His dogs lay growling at his feet. 'That fence may look secure enough now!' he said scornfully. 'But I'd bet my life that goat will have it down within the week!'

Mandy couldn't take any more. She flew down the track to join Lydia. 'Ernie Bell's fence is built to last!' she cried. 'And you've no right to come here threatening people. You! I could report you to the RSPCA!'

She felt James at her shoulder and she could hear her mother's voice trying to calm her down, but she could only think of Houdini lying in agony in Sam Western's yard, near death.

Mr Western's face turned thunderous. 'And I'll have you arrested for trespassing!' he stormed, 'if ever I catch you two on my land again!'

'You poisoned Lydia's goat!' Mandy shouted. 'You poisoned a perfectly innocent goat!' Never in her life had she felt so angry.

He shook his head and waved his hand towards her as if swatting a fly. 'Prove it,' he said quietly.

By now Mr Hope had joined them and Lydia had taken firm hold of Mandy's hand. 'I think it's time to calm down,' he said. 'Nevertheless, I don't like the sound of what happened over at the Hall. An animal like this doesn't rip an entire branch off, as I understand was the case. No, he'll nibble small mouthfuls of the leaf quite happily, without realising the damage he's doing to himself, but he wouldn't wrench off half a bush!' Mr Hope's voice was calm, his gaze was steady. 'It does sound quite deliberate to me, as if somebody intended to do harm!'

Mandy glared. James muttered under his breath.

Sam Western backed off ever so slightly. 'That's

ridiculous!' he said. But his voice had lost its bluster. 'That's quite ridiculous!'

Mr Hope pressed on. 'The RSPCA would take a dim view, I know that.' James and Mandy silently cheered him on. What a hero!

By now Mr Western's resistance had melted. He knew when he was beaten. He'd come up to steamroller Lydia with threats and had met a stone wall of defence for her and her goats. All he had left was a splutter of spite. 'Well, I never expected to find a trained man like you, Hope, up in the wilds defending an old goat woman who couldn't pay a vet's bill to save her life!'

Lydia's head went up. She looked just like Houdini at his most scornful. But she wouldn't lower herself by answering back.

'I'd never have believed it. And of course when I talk to my friends about this, I'll be suggesting they take their business elsewhere, to a vet with a bit more common sense. And that'll be the end of you lot at Animal Ark!'

They stood their ground.

'Don't worry,' Mr Hope whispered to Mandy. 'We're much too well-known in the district to let that sort of threat bother us!'

Mandy nodded.

Sam Western stormed off, the two stocky white dogs

to heel, swishing with his stout stick at the flower heads in the lane. 'Don't think you've heard the last of me!' he shouted as his parting shot.

They stood and stared at his broad back. Mandy still felt a little afraid. Perhaps he could still do Lydia and Animal Ark some damage.

Only Houdini dared treat him with the contempt he deserved. He put back his head, opened his mouth and filled the air with a deafening, mocking bray.

Eight

It was a busy day at Animal Ark. Mrs Walker brought in Joey, her budgie, when he looked a bit off-colour, and James's new neighbour brought in a pet rabbit who was off his food.

'It's probably the move. He doesn't like his routine being altered,' Mrs Hope suggested. 'Give him lots of fresh air and clean water, and don't alter his diet at all at the moment. He's had enough changes.' She popped the little black rabbit back into his basket. 'Come and see me again in a few days if you're still worried.'

The silent, pale little girl who owned the rabbit nodded solemnly and walked out. The basket was nearly as big as her.

'Who's next?' Mrs Hope asked Mandy.

'There's a whole waiting-room full!' Mandy told her. 'Jean's telling people to come back tomorrow rather than wait now, unless it's an emergency.' She showed in a black and white collie with a bad case of flea-bites. 'We're even busier than usual,' she said with a grin.

Mrs Hope checked the sore skin on the dog's back and prescribed some tablets for Simon to make up. Then she washed her hands. 'Yes, your father was right. I don't think we need pay any attention to Sam Western's threats.'

Mandy smiled and went on scrubbing the surfaces of the tables, ready for the next patients.

At school next day she told James how busy they were at Animal Ark. They were ignoring their English lesson — a study of how advertisements work.

'Amanda, I hope you're discussing the advert I've given to you!' Mr Meldrum said in a warning tone of voice.

Mandy blushed and started to concentrate on her coloured picture advertising French perfume. James grinned.

Mr Meldrum walked up and down the aisles between the desks, chuntering on. 'Image is very important,' he said. He stopped by Mandy's desk. 'Take this perfume ad, for instance. The target market here is young women between eighteen and about thirty. And this!' He picked up James's picture of a man on an exercise bike. 'This is for people who want to stay fit and young for ever. That's all of us, I suppose!'

The class laughed politely. But the phrase pierced Mandy's brain with stunning suddenness. 'People who want to stay fit and young for ever . . .'

Mr Meldrum went and sat on his desk, hands in pockets. 'Now, I want you to think of a product of your own to sell. Right? Who's your typical customer going to be? Young, old; married, single? What's the image for your product? Cheap and cheerful; exclusive and sophisticated? What's going to be your main marketing tactic? You have to think about all these angles. Right, off you go!'

There was no need to say another word — Mandy was off. Her product was goats' milk! Her market was the fitness and health food market. Her customers were all those millions of joggers, slimmers, runners, and tennis-players to whom youth and beauty mattered.

'High Cross Goats' Milk. Nature's Best!' That was her slogan. 'High quality drink to aid digestion and improve your skin. Drink goats' milk and live longer!' Suddenly she'd got the next idea for her Save High Cross Farm campaign!

'Good,' Mr Meldrum said over her shoulder. 'But you can't say this about living longer. It may not be true.'

Mandy told him about the man in Asia Minor who lived to be one hundred and eighty.

'Hmm,' he said. 'You could use that story as background to your product, but you can't state definitely that it makes you live longer, OK?'

Mandy nodded and scribbled on. But she wasn't thinking about a classroom advertising assignment. She was thinking of Lydia.

They would need cartons to package the milk and the price of those would have to be considered. They'd need somewhere to sell it. High Cross itself was too far out of town for passing trade . . .

Then Mandy had another flash of inspiration: they could sell the cartons of milk from local health food shops! If she could sell Lydia's milk at a good rate per pint, that could double Lydia's present income! Mandy's eyes lit up. At present Lydia sold her milk very cheaply to the cheese-maker in Thirsk. She was sure she could get a much better price from the health food shops!

Again she rushed to get it all down on paper. She was so busy she didn't even hear the bell go.

At home time she met up with James as usual and they began their cycle ride to Welford.

' "High Cross Goats' Milk. Nature's Best!" '
James listened and nodded. 'Great. And I like your
idea about the health food shops in Walton. It's good!
They'd take goats' milk, especially if they can say it's
local farm produce. Perhaps Simon or your dad would
help us take it round. Just a few pints a day, to see how
it goes!'

They were bubbling with exciting ideas. If Lydia
had six milking goats in the herd at any one time, each
producing up to a gallon of milk a day, the profits
could be really high!

'Less the cost of cartons,' Mandy reminded James.
He was the maths genius. 'We'd have to take that into
account.'

James agreed. 'But Lydia can fix a price and still
make good money,' he said.

'Much more than she earns now!' Mandy grinned.
They freewheeled down the last slope into the village.
'See you tomorrow!' she yelled, swerving sideways
down the drive to Animal Ark.

Lydia proved to be as good at maths as James. She
listened carefully. Yes, she said, it was worth a try!

'I have been a little slow to keep pace with modern
prices,' she admitted. 'I've been so busy just looking
after the goats! I think I would have to buy a fridge,
wouldn't I?'

Mandy nodded. 'But if this works, you won't have to struggle through the winters without food any more!'

'We think it will work!' James insisted. 'You'll have much more money. Maybe you'd even be able to afford a TV!'

'Oh!' Lydia laughed. 'I don't think that would be quite me!'

'Or a phone, at least!' Mandy felt excited at the new prospects for Lydia.

'Ah, well, perhaps a telephone,' she agreed. 'Yes, a telephone might be very nice indeed!'

At home Mandy talked non-stop about their latest plan. 'All Lydia needs is a bit of extra help to set her up,' she explained.

'I wish her well,' Mrs Hope said. 'She's the sort of person I really admire — independent, honest, all those old-fashioned virtues. A real daleswoman!'

'And a good goatkeeper!' Mr Hope added. 'Tell her I'll help whenever I can with transporting the milk to the shops.'

'Oh, thanks, Dad!' Mandy said. Things were working out better than even she had hoped.

Even the health food shops welcomed Lydia with open arms. Yes, said the owner of the Green Health Food

Shop in Walton; and yes, too, from Boswell's Delicatessen. They'd give it a go, small quantities at first. Say a dozen pints a day.

Only Mr Wintersgill, the cheese man from Thirsk, looked glum. Lydia was the only farmer to sell her milk to him so cheaply. Other people charged much more, even in summer.

He stood in the yard at High Cross, hands in pockets. 'Well, I wish you luck,' he told Lydia. 'You and your young business team here.'

Mandy and James smiled.

'Business is business,' said Mr Wintersgill, shaking each of them by the hand. 'I can see you want to modernise, and good luck to you!'

Lydia smiled. 'Thank you. Yes, you're right, this is the idea of my young friends here, and I feel inclined to give them their heads since they've helped me along so nicely through this last terrible winter!'

Mandy and James smiled. This was the world of business and high finance. They felt very important. Even Mr Meldrum, when he saw the green and white carton design and looked at the business plan, congratulated them. 'I'm most impressed! This will look very good on your Personal Action Plan, Amanda!'

Three weeks later they were well underway and the system was working perfectly. Lydia kept her accounts in an old-fashioned ledger, writing in lovely copperplate handwriting. The profits column soon began to show that extra winter feed for the goats was possible. 'For the first time ever!' Lydia exclaimed.

Mandy gave a satisfied sigh. To hear Lydia herself say that next winter would be easier for her and the goats gave her a terrific thrill. She'd put lots of energy into getting the extra food, the fence and the better income from the milk. And now Lydia was saying she wouldn't have to give in to the cruel winters! Mandy looked at her friend's happy face and smiled.

Lydia linked arms and walked out of the barn with her into the fresh air. Mandy had come up early to High Cross, leaving her father to finish one of his training runs alone. They were strolling across the yard, talking about the spring show the following week, when Mandy came to a sudden halt. 'You look different, Lydia!' she said. She'd been too busy talking to notice anything, but now she stood there. She couldn't hide her amazement.

'What?' Lydia smoothed her hair and looked down at herself.

Gone was the mud-brown jacket with the string bunched around the waist by way of a belt. Gone were the torn old wellington boots. In their place Lydia wore a smart royal blue anorak with green lapels and zips and practical pockets everywhere, plus a pair of new green wellies.

'That looks very nice!' Mandy said.

Lydia nodded and said, 'Thank you.' She held her head stiffly, at a slightly backwards slant. She didn't like to talk about how she looked. But Mandy caught her sneaking a glance at her own reflection in the farmhouse window as they passed by. Mandy smiled secretly. Things were certainly changing for the better at High Cross!

It might have been coincidence that Ernie Bell came up to High Cross that day, but Mandy doubted it.

'I'm just here to spread muck in the bottom field,' he explained to Mandy. 'Helping out a bit, that's all!' He coughed and shuffled off across the yard.

Mandy nodded. She didn't dare say anything.

However, it certainly was no coincidence that Ernie's energetic muckspreading took place on the very afternoon of Sam Western's annual garden party.

As the limousines glided through the Hall gates and the guests in suits and hats stepped out and headed for the striped marquee, their nostrils were filled with the rich, sweet-sour smell of fresh manure!

Lydia's bottom field adjoined Sam Western's famous garden, and the wind was in exactly the right direction. Ernie forked the manure off the back of the tractor with great gusto. Sam Western stood at the boundary wall, purple with anger.

'Afternoon!' Ernie said pleasantly to Mr Western and his guests.

Mr Western fumed. The men turned up their noses at the disgusting smell, and several of the ladies nearly fainted. Mandy stood upwind of the tractor, enjoying every second.

'Here now,' Lydia said, striding down towards Mandy in her new boots. 'There's no time for you to be standing here idle.'

Mandy jumped to. 'What's the next job?' she asked, scooting back up the hill.

Lydia seemed to be smiling to herself. 'For once,' she said, 'I've been doing a little planning of my own!'

'What do you mean?' Mandy asked, mystified. She followed Lydia into the barn.

The goats stood contentedly in their pens waiting to be milked. Houdini and Monty chewed away at the latest load of broccoli from the supermarket. Lydia seemed to enjoy her secret as she sat and began milking Lady Jayne.

'Of course, you know that it's the spring show very soon,' she began. 'Well, I've been giving it a certain amount of thought.'

Mandy, sitting alongside in the next pen with Olivia, was dying with curiosity. 'What? What have you been planning, Lydia!'

The milk flowed nicely. 'I've made a decision,'

Lydia said slowly, 'and I'm asking. How would you like to get young Monty ready for the show?'

Mandy gasped. 'You mean, show him myself?'

Lydia nodded. 'If you would like to. There's a good goatling section every year. No doubt there'll be strong competition. But Monty's a fine little goat. I don't see why you shouldn't enter him!' She peered sideways at Mandy.

'You mean, groom him, and get him ready, and take him into the show ring?' Mandy could hardly believe her ears. 'Oh, Lydia, that would be great!' she said.

Nine

'I know, why don't we sell milk and cheese at the show as well?' Mandy exclaimed. She and James were spreading fresh straw in the goats' pens the following day. It seemed the obvious next step in raising Lydia's profits.

'Great idea!' James agreed.

'I'm not so sure,' Lydia protested. 'There'll be a big crowd at the show. I'm not quite used to all those people.'

But Mandy and James gradually convinced her. 'It's a proper farm show!' Mandy said. 'There are the animals and the produce competitions, and some proper local crafts. My grandad's entering his leeks as usual, and there's the big flower tent!'

'It's too good a chance to miss,' James insisted.

'Very well,' Lydia agreed. 'A milk and cheese stall!'

'Great! We'll help, of course!' Mandy and James cried.

But most of Mandy's week went into feeding Monty the best fruit and greens from the supermarket supply and turning him out regularly on to the best spring pasture. The show was only days away and she could think of little else.

She groomed, trimmed and pampered Monty. She put a mineral lick in his pen to tone him up, she provided bucketfuls of fresh spring water.

'You,' she told Monty, 'are going to be the best-turned-out goat for miles around!'

He was a dark-faced goat with shiny, alert eyes. The bloom on his black coat was lovely. No trace of the coarse, dry winter hair was left and everything about him, from well-trimmed hooves to shiny wet nose, showed he was in tip-top condition.

'You'll make Houdini jealous, showering young Monty with all this attention!' Lydia warned.

Mandy grinned. She knew Lydia still had a soft spot for the wicked wanderer.

Houdini stood at a haughty distance from them in the newly-fenced field. Monty, free at last from Mandy's grooming comb, ran and frisked in the long grass. From a distance Mandy could admire his good points. The judges at the show would be looking for a strong, straight back, depth of chest, fine legs. 'Do you think he has a chance of winning?' Mandy asked.

Lydia eyed him shrewdly. 'He's a good little goat,' was all she was prepared to say.

They went back up to the farm together to work in the dairy. There was milk to be put in cartons, and an experiment in making soft cheese for the produce stall. 'We still have to check the special health regulations,' Lydia said, 'and I must make sure of the arrangements to transport the milk and cheese down to the showground when Saturday comes.'

'Did Ernie Bell manage to borrow a van for the day?' Mandy asked.

'Yes, and he tells me he's knocked together a large trestle-table for the stall.' Lydia bustled about, flushed and nervous. 'I must say, I'm still not looking forward to the day,' she admitted, shaking her head.

'It's the only trestle-table I've ever seen with dovetail joints,' Mr Hope commented as he helped unload the beautifully made thing at the showground on the Friday night.

'Aye, well, when I do a job I like to do it properly,' Ernie said, secretly pleased. 'Tell Miss Fawcett I'll be

up early tomorrow morning with the van,' he told
Mandy.

'Seven o'clock?' she asked. She knew what he
meant by 'early'.

'On the dot,' Ernie said. 'We've got a lot of setting
up to do.'

Mandy looked back and waved as she left the
showground. There were trailers unloading bales of
straw and marquees half-erected. Her gran was
already organising the Women's Institute refreshment
tent, and her grandad was setting out neat labels for
the vegetable section. This would be a great event; a
farm show which attracted farmers from this dale and
the next, with its huge tents, its show rings, its fell race
and flower competitions. Excitement was already
building up. Mandy got the first real flutterings of
nerves as she turned and rode off.

She cycled up to High Cross to put the finishing
touches to Monty, and to help with the evening
milking. The sun, low on the horizon, cast long, warm
shadows on the grey farmhouse. The windows and
doors all stood open. Mandy could see Lydia running
from house to barn and across to the cool house with
great buckets of creamy milk. Her face, glowing in the
sun, opened up into a smile when she saw Mandy.
'Come here!' she beckoned.

She took her out into the field. Houdini was

showing off in front of the female goats. He pranced up and down along the top wall. His audience gazed spellbound at his tricks. He skipped on to the wall top to perform a fine tightrope walking act without dislodging a single stone.

'Of course, he's still a bit mad about the new fence,' Lydia explained, as Houdini butted his head against the chain link enclosure. 'It cramps his style, I think you'd say!'

'But even Houdini can't climb that!' Mandy laughed.

'Touch wood!' Lydia dashed for the nearest fencepost.

'But where's Monty?'

'Ah!' Lydia paused awkwardly. 'Houdini's got himself into a spot of bother there!'

And again she beckoned Mandy, this time out of the field and into the barn. 'I thought I'd better put Monty in here out of harm's way until you came,' she explained on Houdini's behalf. And she pointed to a very sorry sight.

Monty stood dejected in his pen. His bright coat, his lovely bright coat, was covered from head to foot in brown, matted, foul-smelling, dried-out manure! He looked sorrowfully at Mandy and gave her a feeble bleat.

'What happened!' Mandy was shocked. Was this

the goat she was supposed to take to the show tomorrow?

'Houdini, that's what happened!' Lydia apologised. 'I warned you he'd get jealous. Well, he caught poor little Monty when my back was turned for a second just as I'd finished milking this morning. I was letting the herd out to pasture. He must have cornered Monty in the yard and bundled him straight into the manure heap! No mercy, you see — just a quick shove to teach him who's boss!'

'Oh!' Mandy stood and shook her head.

'Bit of a mess, isn't he?' Lydia said. 'And feeling very sorry for himself!'

Mandy talked nicely to Monty until he stopped bleating. She considered several clean-up tactics — the hose down, the buckets of soapy water. But goats hate being wet and can sulk for days. She didn't want Monty trailing down to the show looking miserable. That would spoil any chance they had of winning a prize. There was no way round it — out came the grooming comb. Carefully, strand by strand, she untangled the horrid, smelly mess!

Two hours later he was clean as any model in a shampoo advert. Her arms felt as if they were about to drop off, but Monty was clean! Head up, frisky, graceful little Monty — as good as new!

'Well done,' Lydia nodded.

Mandy breathed out noisily. 'Just keep him away from Houdini for the night, will you!' she said.

She cycled home, went straight to bed, and fell into an exhausted sleep.

But she was up with the dawn, racing to draw back the curtains to check the sky. Would it be fine for the show? Would it rain and spoil everything?

A few clouds drifted across a mainly blue sky and there had been a shower during the night. The ground was still damp. But Mandy scrambled into clean shorts and T-shirt, daring the weather to be anything but sunny. Then she had to do her chores at Animal Ark in double-quick time, and help cope with two emergencies before surgery.

'Go on,' her mum said, glancing at the clock. 'Simon's due any minute. We can cope here if you want to get off up to High Cross.'

Mandy was out of the door and halfway up the drive before she'd finished the sentence.

Ernie was already there, loading milk and cheese into the borrowed Transit van. He'd hired a refrigerating unit from a butcher friend and was showing Lydia how it would keep the produce cool throughout the day. She smiled like a child at Christmas. 'Wonderful!' she repeated over and over. She kept on running back into the house for her accounts book, her loose change, her 'Nature's Best' signs, her jacket in case it rained.

For a moment Mandy thought she might even change her mind completely. It was a big day for Lydia. This would be the first time she'd been down from High Cross to sell her milk and meet her customers. 'Come on,' Mandy said. 'There's no need to worry.'

But Lydia looked doubtful. 'I'm sure you could manage without me,' she protested. 'Why don't I stay up here to mind Houdini and the rest?'

Ernie sat in the driver's seat and shook his head. 'Don't be daft!' he said. 'We need you. You're the goat lady, remember!'

Something about his tone of voice made Lydia pull herself together. She swallowed hard and nodded. 'Right then, we're all set!' She got into the van and spoke to Mandy before she closed the door. 'Remember to check Houdini one last time before you leave!'

Mandy nodded and waved the red van off down the track, full to the brim with Nature's Best produce. There was Monty to see to − a final brush, a quick polish of the hooves, a comb of the straggly beard. Then her dad drove up to see if she was ready. It was ten-thirty and he was already in his track suit for the start of the fell race at eleven-fifteen.

'Nervous?' he asked Mandy, who led Monty carefully up the ramp into the Land-rover.

'Yes,' she said. 'Are you?'

'Yes.'

'Let's go then. I've got to meet James in fifteen minutes.'

Mandy even remembered to see that Houdini was safe in the top field with the other goats before they drove off. She gave him an apple through the wire fence. 'That's right, good boy!'

Houdini caught sight of smart little Monty peering out of the back of the Land-rover. He snickered with envy from behind his prison wall.

'Poor old Houdini!' Mandy felt genuinely sorry for him.

'Is he feeling left out?' Mr Hope asked as they drove off.

She nodded. 'It's a shame!'

Mandy turned and saw Houdini glaring angrily at the disappearing Land-rover.

But village life in all its splendour greeted them at the show field behind the church and Mandy was instantly caught up in it. She forgot Houdini and concentrated on Monty, taking him from the Land-rover and tethering him alongside the other goats — fawn Toggenburgs, white Saanens, other black and white

Alpines — all splendidly turned out and dapper.

Mandy's heart sank a bit, but she sweet-talked Monty into staying put on his running tether. 'Now, Monty, it's not going to rain on you and there's plenty of juicy grass within reach. Just stay here and be a good boy!'

She checked the chain one last time. Other owners were making last minute preparations too, but many were wandering off across the show ring to glance at other events before the judging began.

Confident there would be no trouble, Mandy left the animal compound and went off to the main arena with its huge marquee and all the craft and produce stalls. It was eleven-fifteen — time for the start of the fell race. As her dad's official trainer it was her duty to cheer him on!

Mandy's gran was doing great business on the cake stall, and her grandad was dispensing cups of hot tea. Behind them, the garden experts were carrying their prize exhibits into the flower tent — huge begonias and perfect roses, arrangements of lilies, ferns in bottles. Mandy caught sight of Sam Western, showing off as usual about his unique type of rose, explaining its advantages to anyone who would listen. 'I've called it Cream Surprise!' he said, disappearing inside the tent with it as if it were an endangered species.

Outside there was a nice bustling crowd round the

craft and produce stalls. A man was sitting cross-legged making willow baskets by the traditional method and Mandy was astonished to learn that he was blind. There were corn-dollie stalls, patchwork quilt stalls, and there, extra busy and doing great business, was the High Cross Farm Produce Stall. Nature's Best. Mandy gave Lydia and Ernie a wave, met up with an excited James, and scooted off to the far side of the arena, where the brass band had just finished and the fell racers were lining up for the start.

Mandy and James, already hot and sticky under the cloudless sky, gave Mr Hope a thumbs up.

'He looks very lean and fit,' James said, sounding surprised.

'James says you look lean and fit!' she yelled, and her dad grinned and gave back a cheery thumbs up. 'And so he ought to,' she said to James, 'after all the training I've put into this!'

'Here's your mum,' James said. And the three of them stood at the start line, ready to yell when the gun went off.

'Ready, steady . . .' the starter shouted and fired his raised pistol.

A gaggle of men and women, young and old, scrawny and stocky, plus a few children, set off up the field.

The trio from Animal Ark watched them bunch

over the road and begin to string out up the nursery slopes of the grey and green fell. Soon they were practically out of sight. They looked like colourful little ants on a quick route-march up an impossible hill.

'Let's have a cup of tea,' Mrs Hope suggested, 'before the judging.' She looked at Mandy. 'Come on, it'll calm your nerves!'

But Mandy only lasted two minutes in the tea tent before she was off back to the animal compound, untethering Monty and fussing him as the judges made their slow progress towards them. She combed him for the twentieth time that morning, and tweaked his beard into perfect shape.

Monty bore it all like a veteran.

The judges were a small man in a natty tweed hat and jacket, and a tall grey-haired woman in a white coat. When their turn came at last, Mandy led Monty out into the centre of the little judging circle. The tweedy man stood sideways, frontways, and then took position at Monty's back end. He ticked boxes on a sheet. The grey-haired woman looked intently in Monty's mouth, checked his ears, felt the texture of his coat. 'Good feet,' Mandy heard her say to her fellow judge. 'Would you walk him for us?'

Mandy clicked her tongue and walked Monty along. He held his head high and lifted his feet daintily. He seemed to know he was on show. There was a spring in his stride and a knowing look in his eye. 'Good boy, Monty!' Mandy breathed.

The judges conferred. They ticked more boxes. The severe lady smiled. 'Thank you very much!' she said, and they moved on to the next competitor.

Mandy held her breath. She gave Monty a quick hug. 'Well done!' she said, for he'd behaved like the perfect goat.

'Well?' James came up and asked impatiently.

'I don't know. We'll have to wait.'

In the distance the colourful runners were scrambling back down the hillside, one and two at a time like a string of bright beads. The fell race was in its final stages and Mandy was torn between running over to cheer on her dad in the final leg, or staying put for the judges' verdict on Monty. The wait was endless as still they passed on from goat to goat. And the fell racers got nearer and nearer.

'Hey, your dad's near the front! There, in the blue!' James yelled. He ran over to the finishing line for a better view.

But Mandy couldn't leave Monty. He skipped and skittered on the end of the tether. She put an arm on his neck. The judges were coming back! The tweedy man was taking rosettes out of his pocket; yellow, red and blue. The woman was announcing the winners.

'Third prize, Pearl-Barley!' she said loud and clear.

The pure Toggenburg goat and its proud owner stepped up to receive the yellow rosette.

'Second prize, Old Moore!'

Mandy bit her lip. She could hardly bear to look. The red rosette was pinned on the collar of a lovely cream coloured Saanen with pink ears and nose. The owner grinned from ear to ear.

'And first prize, for a really lovely little goat,' the lady announced, pausing for breath, 'Monty from High Cross Farm!'

There was a burst of applause and smiling faces. Monty moved beside Mandy at a sprightly pace. They went up to the judges to receive his blue rosette. There was shaking of hands and warm compliments.

'Well done!' Everyone crowded round with their congratulations. Mandy flung her arms round Monty and kissed him. She hugged the silky blue rosette to her chest. Still she could hardly believe it!

In a daze she returned Monty to his tether. 'Wait here,' she told him. 'Be a good boy. I have to go and tell the others!'

The crowd roared as she charged across the arena, but not for her. The fell racers were in the final sprint. She held up her blue rosette. 'Come on, Dad, you can do it!' She waved and yelled frantically, along with James and Mrs Hope.

Mr Hope put his shoulders back and lengthened his stride. He was fourth! He passed one, then two runners whose legs had begun to go. He gritted his teeth. The leaders' chests were heaving, in spite of the cheers. But Mr Hope pressed forwards, pushing for the finishing tape.

He was just behind the leader, the runner in black! One metre, one and a half metres behind! They both fell over the tape to a mighty cheer. Second! Mr Hope was second! He bent double, clutching the red rosette.

'Dad, Dad!' Mandy rushed forward. 'We won! Monty and I won!' She waved the fluttering blue rosette in front of him.

Mr Hope looked up and grinned. He grabbed her round the waist, lifted her off her feet and swung her

round. He made a yell like a Scottish dancer. And
James and Mrs Hope came and joined in their little jig
of victory.

'Let's go and tell Lydia!' Mandy said, breathless
with delight.

She pushed through the crowd to reach the stall and
thrust the blue rosette into Lydia's hands. 'It's yours!'
she said. 'Monty was absolutely brilliant!'

Lydia beamed. 'So Monty did it after all!' She
hugged Mandy. 'Well done! Well done, you two.' She
hung the blue rosette in pride of place on the High
Cross stall. 'We've taken one hundred and thirty-six
pounds and fifteen pence!' she said proudly. 'And
people have been so kind!'

'She never knew she was so famous, with her goats
tucked up on the hill,' Ernie said. 'And folks have
come and put in regular orders for the cheese. They
say they swear by goats' milk and cheese. But up till
now it's been hard to get hold of!'

'A real success!' Mrs Hope said, her face sharing
everyone else's delight. 'Record profits for the farm!
Rosettes everywhere, and everybody happy!'

'A perfect day!' Mandy agreed.

Ten

There was chaos in the flower tent! People were yelling, and tables were falling and crashing. Two ladies in pink flowered hats shot out of the exit. Mandy recognised Mrs Ponsonby, her gran's chief rival in the Women's Institute, rushing to safety with Pandora and Toby, her two precious dogs.

'Help! Help! He tried to eat my hat!' squealed one.

Burly men in checked shirts and jeans ran inside, but soon emerged looking shellshocked and helpless. 'He's going mad in there!' one said, rubbing his backside. But even now, some were beginning to grin.

'Who is?' James left the others rooted to the spot

and ran up to one of the men.

'Somebody's goat's got loose, gone on the rampage. He's eating all the flowers!' the man said.

But Mandy didn't wait to hear any more. 'Houdini!' she gasped with a dreadful certainty.

'Are you sure?' Mr Hope said. 'How did he get out?'

The crashes and yells inside the great marquee continued. 'Stop that goat!' someone roared.

Lydia listened, horrified. 'He must have climbed the fence,' she said weakly.

'He couldn't!' Mandy objected. 'It's too high!'

'He must have done it somehow. If one of the goats, say Lady Jayne, stood on the wall top, Houdini could sort of piggyback on to her and then spring over the top.'

'Never!' Ernie said.

'Oh, yes,' Mr Hope agreed. 'It's perfectly possible. Remember, goats live on mountainsides. They can reach impossible places just for a blade of grass!'

'And a goat like Houdini can perform miracles!' Lydia said, her voice failing, her face worried.

Mandy looked at James. James looked at Mandy. 'Well?' she said.

'Ready!' he replied.

Together they sprinted for the entrance to the tent. Inside, every table was overturned. There were

flowers everywhere: lilies, geraniums, begonias, roses! White, yellow and brilliant red. They were strewn all over the grass and trampled. They were half eaten and torn apart. White tablecloths were trodden in the turf, flower vases lay on their sides trickling water. A brave head or two peered up from behind a table where people had barricaded themselves, hats askew, looks of horror on their faces.

'My rose! My perfect rose!' a deep voice roared, louder than all the rest. Sam Western stood astride a broken table brandishing his fist. 'My beautiful Cream Surprise!'

The goat stood ten metres away, head up, front hoof pawing the grass. A black goat. A fine, strong British Alpine with a glint in his eye. Houdini! And in his mouth he held the thorny stems of George Western's prize rose. The blooms trembled dangerously on the end of their stems. 'Save my roses!' Mr Western thundered. 'Stop that goat!'

A single Cream Surprise fluttered to the ground. Houdini trampled it. He shook the bunch of flowers and petals rained down. He tossed his head, opened his mouth, and ruined flower heads fell everywhere.

'Oh!' groaned Mr Western.

'Houdini!' Mandy shouted.

The goat's attention was distracted for a moment. He recognised her voice and turned. He trotted a pace or two towards her in greeting. But her tone of voice made him hesitate.

'Wicked boy!' she said, advancing slowly, James by her side.

Then Sam Western did precisely the wrong thing. He jumped down clumsily from the broken table and galloped towards his ruined roses. Even now he tried to snatch them from Houdini's path. He bent to pick them up.

But Houdini turned. He'd seen the man run towards the flowers. He put his head down and revved up with his back legs, sounding like a racing car raring to go. Then he shot forwards. Mandy watched, horrified, as the man's corduroy-trousered backside reared up in front of Houdini.

Goat's horns met man's buttocks with a terrific thud. Sam Western was pitched forwards five metres towards the toppled tables. He fell heavily, face down, dragging tablecloths and flowers with him in a chaotic heap.

Houdini bent calmly and nipped with his rubbery pink lips at every last rose. He curled his tongue round each one and savoured the taste of each prize petal. He didn't even mind when Mandy and James approached him, one on either side, and Mandy slipped a rope round his neck.

'Naughty boy!' Mandy said, as severely as she could.

James ran over to help Mr Western to his feet. 'Get off!' Sam Western bawled. 'Fetch the police! Goat on the loose!'

More heads popped up out of hiding to see Mandy steadily leading Houdini towards the exit. Mr Western was waving his arms like a windmill, while James tried in vain to brush him down.

'This goat is a menace! He must be stopped! Call the police!' Mr Western yelled, beside himself with rage. 'Come along there! Don't just let them escape!' He barked orders at the gardening experts slowly emerging from their hiding-places.

Mandy bit her lip and prayed they could reach the exit before anyone pounced. 'Come on, boy!' she whispered. 'Please don't get up to any of your nonsense right now!'

Houdini trotted obediently on.

'Well, don't just stand there!' Mr Western roared.

But everyone did. 'Who does he think he is?' Mrs Ponsonby muttered, peering inside the tent when she heard George Western's angry shouts. 'Giving all the orders!'

'Blooming lord of the manor!' someone else replied sarcastically.

Men folded their strong, tanned forearms across their chests and stood wide-legged, refusing to budge.

Mandy and Houdini made the exit. A blast of hot,

sunny air met them, and a dazzling light.

Lydia ran forward the moment she saw them. 'Houdini!' She spoke so severely that even he hung his head in shame.

'Don't tell him off!' Mandy pleaded. 'He was only going after what he saw as a treat!'

'That's right,' Mrs Ponsonby agreed. 'It's only natural for a goat.' She fixed her hat and her glasses firmly on, fussed with her hair to put everything straight. But she was on Mandy's side in spite of the fright Houdini had given her. 'It's high time Sam Western was taken down a peg or two!' she announced.

Mandy stared. She waited for the verdict from the rest of the crowd.

Others nodded. 'You must admit, it has its funny side! Goat Gobbles Prize Flowers! We'll be dining out on this one till Christmas!' They laughed among themselves.

'Did you see the way he butted Sam Western?' someone said, and described it again in full detail. Soon everyone roared with laughter.

'Just a bit of harmless fun,' they all agreed.

No amount of ordering, threatening and arm waving from Sam Western as he emerged from the tent would alter things. Houdini, no longer the villain of the flower tent, was fast becoming the hero of the whole show! Sam Western stood and fumed in vain.

Mandy grinned at James. She still held Houdini on a tight rein and when her mum came up and whispered that now was the time to make a quick exit, Mandy nodded. 'We'll all stay here and help Lydia finish off at the stall,' said Mrs Hope. 'And don't worry about Monty — we'll bring him home in the Land-rover. Now you head off with this old rascal while the going's good!'

Mandy led Houdini, cheerful as ever, through the crowd. He'd never been in better spirits. One or two people applauded as he passed. 'Quite a celebrity, that goat,' someone said loudly. Mandy felt a bit like a queen, all eyes on her and Houdini.

'Wait!' James said, going with her across the open arena. He shot over to the High Cross stall and came back with Monty's blue rosette. 'Lydia says Houdini can wear it. After all, he's Monty's dad. Without Houdini none of this would have happened!'

'You can say that again!' And she proudly stuck the rosette through the rope around Houdini's neck. She could have sworn he winked at her as they left the arena through the main gate.

She turned just once to wave at Lydia. But Lydia stood by her nearly empty stall, hands in pockets, staring up at the fellside. She was thinking her own happy thoughts.

Mandy and Houdini chatted all the way home. It took half an hour on foot; past the church, through the back way by the Fox and Goose, up the hill towards the Beacon. The shadows lengthened. A pink tinge came into the sky. A breeze rustled the meadows which shone like silvery green silk.

They took their time. Houdini even paused to look nosily through the bars of Mr Western's garden gate as they passed by.

'Uh-oh!' Mandy put on a burst of speed, dragging Houdini after. 'Not again!'

'I'm just looking!' Houdini seemed to say, with a little shake of his head. The blue rosette fluttered.

The farm was in sight. Home for Houdini. He didn't complain as Mandy opened the gate into the top field. Olivia came trotting up to say hello. Two of the kids fell over each other to join in the greeting. 'Go on, tell them about it!' Mandy said, laughing.

For a moment or two she studied the high fence for signs of the escape route. It still seemed impossible, even for a super acrobat and escapologist like Houdini. Soon she gave up wondering. She made one last check that the gate was shut tight and locked. All the goats were safe inside.

Until tomorrow. Who knew what Houdini would be up to tomorrow? Mandy laughed out loud.

How could she be cross with someone as clever as

Houdini? He grazed contentedly by the stream at the very spot where Mandy had first seen Lydia, back in the late snowfall. This was a goat who would get into many more gardens before he was through.

Mandy took one last look. She stood there and wondered how anyone could help but admire Houdini and his amazing escapes!